THE FAKE

Zoe Whittall

THE
FAKE

A NOVEL

HarperCollins*Publishers*Ltd

Published by HarperCollins Publishers Ltd

First edition

HarperCollins books may be purchased for educational, business, or sales promotional
use through our Special Markets Department.

HarperCollins Publishers Ltd
Bay Adelaide Centre, East Tower
22 Adelaide Street West, 41st Floor
Toronto, Ontario, Canada
M5H 4E3

www.harpercollins.ca

Book design by Fritz Metsch

The epigraph on page ix is from "Italo Calvino, The Art of Fiction No. 130," which
appears in the *Paris Review*, Issue 124, Fall 1992, and features selections from
interviews with Calvino by William Weaver and Damien Pettigrew.

Lyrics from the Weakerthans' "Sun in an Empty Room" by
John K. Samson used with permission.

Library and Archives Canada Cataloguing in Publication
Title: The fake : a novel / Zoe Whittall. Names: Whittall, Zoe, author.
Identifiers: Canadiana (print) 20220443564 | Canadiana (ebook) 20220443580 ISBN
9781443455275 (hardcover) | ISBN 9781443455282 (softcover)
ISBN 9781443455299 (EPUB) Classification: LCC PS8595.H4975 F35 2023
DDC C813/.6—dc23

Printed and bound in the United States of America
23 24 25 26 27 LBC 5 4 3 2 1

For Paulie

Thanks for saying yes at that Sleater-Kinney
show in 1998 so that eventually we could survive
a pandemic together

Novelists tell that piece of truth at the bottom of every lie. To a psychoanalyst it is not so important whether you tell the truth or a lie because lies are as interesting, eloquent, and revealing as any claimed truth.

—ITALO CALVINO

THE FAKE

was kidnapped when I was eight years old. I was sitting in the Oldsmobile, the one we called Carla Number 3, with the broken passenger-side door that was held together with bailer twine and bungee cords. You had to get into the car from the driver's side, and the back seat was always full of phone books and old computer parts. So even if I had wanted to jump out, I couldn't. This was back when you could leave kids in cars. In the parking lot of the A&P I likely wasn't the only kid in hand-me-down mittens waiting on an adult who was shooting the shit with Marlene, the only weekday cashier. My dad smoked a cigarette and leaned against the ice machine, the looped handle of a yellow grocery bag tucked around the elbow of his silver ski jacket. Everyone walking in and out of the store looked like they were smoking because it was so cold. He'd left the keys in the car so the heat could run. A guy just got in and drove me away. He said his name was Benjamin. I don't think he wanted a kid, I think he wanted a car. Maybe. I don't remember all that much after he told me his name. I don't remember how I got home. But I do know I lived with my nana for a whole summer after that. She had a little red bungalow halfway between our church and the Chicken Yum Diner. Every night she'd say, *Come on, let's go brush our jimmies.* She'd tuck me into her waterbed with the coral satin sheets and then go sleep on the couch. Nana said my dad was special and the world was never fair to him. In the fall we had to go to court, my sister and I, and say where we wanted to live. My mother let my dad have weekends. Which to him meant once a month.

My childhood was unremarkable, except for the kidnapping. I stayed out of trouble unless you messed with my sister. I graduated with a respectable B average from my tiny high school on the shores of the greatest of the Great Lakes, and I went to college in the city for an English degree. I didn't expect to get knocked up at eighteen, but I guess it's in my genes. I named her Buffy like the slayer and sent her off to live with a nice middle-aged couple in Barrie. That's why I never go to Barrie. I think if I saw her, I would know. But sometimes I get drunk and get on a bus there. I'm sober enough by the time I arrive that I just turn around and come back.

When I was twenty-five, I became best friends with Morgan, the head bartender at an Irish pub on College Street where I was a server. Morgan and me were so tight we spent Christmases together. Nana loved Morgan. We went to Mexico when we conned two rich guys into taking us to an all-inclusive. The strongest woman I ever met. On the night of a citywide blackout, I walked into the storage room and found her dead. They say when you hang yourself you really fucking mean it. She left me a note that just said, *thanks for being loyal.* That's why I've got this tattoo right here.

My boyfriend at the time thought I was in love with Morgan, but that's just because he didn't have any imagination. He was a very literal person. But maybe he realized I didn't really care about him, and he saw that I was capable of caring for someone by how I treated Morgan.

A year later, I found out I had a rare form of cancer. I kept trying to finish school and go to work, though. I'd just gone back to college at night to become a real estate agent. I was turning my life around and then the test results laughed in my face. I wanted life to be as normal as possible, despite the treatments. I told my family I was going to handle it on my own. After Morgan died, my sister died. I started going to this grief support group. I didn't know what else to do. Now it's my home base.

Every Tuesday, we had a fortune-teller come into the bar. Gabriella the Wonder. I would never let her predict anything about me, but the night after my diagnosis I sat down and asked her point-blank, am I cursed?

She put her hands around my face. She smelled like the Tuesday night jalapeño poppers special and our lowest-shelf scotch. She said, *Oh little one, you did something so bad in a past life, you might want to hurry up and get this one over with.*

I laughed it off, but it came back to me on my thirtieth birthday as I loaded my dad's old .22 rifle and put it behind the driver's seat of the pickup and drove into the city to confront the ones who thought they could take everything away from me.

———

Who are you gonna believe? Someone like me, who has survived so much, and has nothing to lose? Or a pathetic man who could barely tie his shoes after his wife left him? Or a woman who always thinks she has a brain tumour and has panic attacks in the grocery store? You're going to believe them because they have perfect teeth and never had to do anything they didn't want to do in life. I am tough because I have had to be.

You're a smart person, obviously. You read books. I'm just trying to give you the basics right now. I have the right to defend myself. Doesn't everyone, even these days?

TODAY

Shelby hides in the closet and calls her father. It's a primal, childlike thing to do, to call your dad when you're in danger. If you have a good father, anyway, and Shelby's is one of the best. Also, she is maybe still a bit drunk, not thinking clearly. Voicemail. He's the kind of dad who insists on singing his outgoing message to the tune of "Born in the U.S.A."—*The Roberstons ARE not HOME! Soooo LEAVE A message at the TONE!*—with her mother's voice in the background telling him to just stop it already.

"I think there's someone in the house. I'm hiding in the closet. Can you come over?" Her heart sprints in place. The dog is no use in this situation. Coach Taylor Swift, a simple-minded but precious rescue pug, is now resting on a tattered quilt in the corner, licking his asshole like nothing is wrong. Shelby pushes the mountain of dirty clothes in front of the closed closet door to block any sound. She rummages around on the stack of boxed shelves above the dog and finds a pair of Kate's ice skates. She pulls off the purple plastic guards around the blades and shines her phone's light on them so she doesn't accidentally cut herself. This could be a weapon. She holds one skate by the ankle. If Kate were still alive, she'd have gotten up and grabbed the bat they kept under the bed and charged

toward the kitchen turning on every light and singing the chorus
to that annoying counting song from *Rent* that somehow sounded
menacing the way she sang it. Shelby always misses Kate but she
especially misses her now, her butch bravado, except when it came
to spiders or wet paper in the sink. Spiders are the femme's
domain, Kate said the day they moved in together, standing on a
kitchen stool after seeing a daddy longlegs hanging out in the
space between the fridge and the wall, ruling over a veritable city
of baby spiders. Though Shelby is afraid of most things, she
doesn't mind spiders. She'd cupped and carried them to the window and set them free into the boxed herb garden as Kate impro-
vised a thank-you song, still safely standing on the stool, fingers
touching the ceiling.

Shelby texts her dad. The message goes green, which means he's
turned on airplane mode to sleep. Of course, her father probably
isn't looking at his cellphone, he still uses it like a walkie-talkie.
She tries the landline again. They don't pick up. She remembers
her parents have gone to the symphony. She went to bed an hour
ago, but other adults who aren't dangerously depressed are still out
having a good time right now. Should she call 911? What if it was
no one? Everyone already thinks she's going crazy. She scrolls
through her contacts. Who are her friends? The ones close enough
to call in moments like this? When you no longer have a partner,
you have to rank your friends in order of most useful in an emergency. Her ICE listing was Kate. Whose phone was currently in a
little Ziploc bag in their shared nightstand with her keys, receipts,
and the contents of her pockets from the day she died. There's
Carol Jo, the person who lives closest, but Shelby had blocked and
deleted her number the week before. So she texts Gibson. *This is
going to sound crazy, but do you know where she is right now? Because
I'm worried she's in my house. She's made some threats.* He calls her

back. She so recently considered him an enemy, someone not to be trusted, that it's still odd to see his name pop up. She puts the phone to her ear and whispers, "I'm hiding in the closet."

"Look, until today I would have said you're overreacting, that she's only a harm to herself, but I honestly don't know what she's capable of anymore. Stay where you are. I'm coming over."

Shelby hangs up. It's very quiet in the house for five agonizing minutes, so quiet she contemplates just going out to see what's really going on. She has a brief, flickering euphoric feeling of *If I die, I die!* Like she does whenever there is in-flight turbulence, or when a taxi driver speeds like a madman through the city and she's too nonconfrontational to say anything. It's a light feeling in her chest, a release of the illusion of control over her circumstances. Then Coach Taylor whines a little. She *has* to stay alive for Coach, a dog with such a complicated daily system of medications and nurturance needed just to be baseline okay. Maybe it's just a raccoon in the garbage—this is Toronto, after all—or a vicious wind in the yard. Perhaps an ordinary robber who is strong-arming her flatscreen and going on his way. She reaches over to scratch Coach's head, which makes them both feel sleepy. Maybe she should just go back to bed. She is lolling into what her therapist calls sensory underwhelm when she hears the sound of gunshots and breaking glass.

1

Gibson is getting head from an enthusiastic woman he met three hours earlier. It's probably the fastest a terrible day has ever turned around. His migraine had finally lifted at noon, which always makes him feel a combination of reborn and disoriented, like he doesn't quite know who he is anymore. He hadn't left his one-bedroom apartment in three days, nor has he unpacked more than two boxes since he moved in the week before. They are all lined up against the one wall in the already too-narrow hallway, across from the staircase that leads to the street-level entrance. He sometimes worries he might pitch over the banister to his death when he gets up to pee at night. It's an apartment that was designed to be the second floor of a family home, with one long hallway and three separate rooms meant to be bedrooms, now badly disguised as an entire apartment. His kitchen is small, at the top of the stairs, with a door to the back patio, then a bathroom meant for children, a small living room that only fits a love seat, and a bedroom that overlooks the street. He's plugged in his TV and the coffee maker and made makeshift chairs out of boxes. His mattress is on the floor, covered in one thin sheet and a sleeping bag. It hurts his knees to stand up every morning.

He only went out because it was Julian's birthday party, in the back room of one of those generic pubs on College Street. His divorce was so recent that he's still in the stage where he has to remember who his friends are and how to be a friend, the way you don't have to when you're married. He can barely remember the kindergarten-level truths about friendship, let alone how to pick up a new lover. Something about being near middle-aged and trying to be more than casual buddies with another guy doesn't make sense.

Gibson knows every blowjob is a good blowjob, but this one makes all the others obsolete. She did all the work at the bar, and she is doing all the work now. He's like a newly hatched chick with a dumb, bewildered look on his face, just happy to be alive. His ex-wife, Veda, was good at them, but one time she let it slip that it hurt her jaw and that it wasn't her favourite activity, so he never let her do it again. That was years ago. When they still had sex.

Before he'd left for Julian's party he'd caught a fleeting glimpse of his naked body in the bathroom mirror and actually started crying. It's been one of those weeks—nay, years—where to let what he looks like truly sink in would be a cruelty to himself. He chooses instead to function as a floating head, dragging a skin sack around behind him, ignoring it. But she chose him, of all the guys in that bar with excellent beards and flat stomachs. And here they are.

There's a warm summer breeze coming in through his bedroom window, as well as the jarring orange glow of a streetlight that usually keeps him awake and cursing his decision not to install proper blinds.

You can tell when a girl gives head because she thinks she should, like it's an item on the list to tick off before actual sex. That's how he remembers it from college anyway, when he had exactly three casual relationships before he met Veda in grad

school. It doesn't make him feel powerful, like it seems to make
other men feel. He feels like a bull's-eye of vulnerability. He likes
to go down on women first; he's polite and also thinks it makes
sense physically to do it in that order. Plus, he's pretty good at it
sometimes, but she didn't give him a chance. And she is obviously
enjoying herself, because she keeps looking up at him and smirk-
ing in a way that is scrambling his brain. He feels seventeen again.
He pulls her up before it becomes impossible. She giggles, pushes
him down on his back, straddling him. She is the director here. He
feels pulled along, but in a good way. Her long brown hair tickles
him, falls around her like an impressive mane. She spreads one
hand across his chest, holds him that way, then pulls her panties
aside and touches herself, giggling. She's got a stick-and-poke tattoo on her inner thigh that says *Heal Me*. Gibson watches her for a
few minutes, until he can tell she's going to come, so he flips her
over so that she's on her back and traces the tattoo with his tongue.

"What's this mean?"

"That I got high with a tattoo gun one night," she says.

He laughs. "Why *Heal Me*? What does it mean?"

Her face gets briefly serious, and then she says, "I know how to
shut you up," as she flips him and straddles his face. Gibson hasn't
been drunk in years, but he is right now, otherwise he'd never have
gone home with a stranger. He did shots like a teenager. Liquid
Cocaine shooters—gold leaf vodka and Jägermeister. Several
times. He drank quickly when he got there because the dankness
of the bar, the stilted conversations with Julian's work friends, and
the smell of draft-soaked carpeting and the sounds of canned Top
40 shit made him want to go home and stick his head in the oven.
He ordered two pints and drank them so quickly he had to keep
turning away from people to belch into the wall.

She was standing at the bar with a thin blond guy. They were both wearing terry-cloth rompers. Hers was red with white piping and was so tight it looked like underwear from certain angles. Before their divorce Veda went through a phase of ordering dozens of these types of one-piece jumpsuits, and he'd made the mistake of telling her—he'd called them playsuits, by mistake—that they looked like they were designed for teenagers. "They are called rompers and it is the height of fashion right now and I was hoping you'd notice I was making an effort!" she'd said. He'd apologized, and even ordered her one when it came across his Instagram feed, but it had been hideously ugly and she never wore it.

But this girl looked like designers made rompers with her body in mind. Her guy friend wore a lime-green one, equally tight, and Gibson wasn't sure if it was supposed to be a joke or a costume, but he tried not to stare either way. He felt worried for the guy, because some of Julian's friends were from way back, from Owen Sound, and they weren't as cool as he and Julian were about gay men. Luckily, he didn't have to intervene on any embarrassing behaviour, and he kept his eyes on the girl in red the drunker he got.

They were the only two people in the place not attending Julian's party. Later he found out she worked there, but it was her night off and she'd come in to get her tips and some beer with her staff discount. He can't believe Julian is forty. Only six months until Gibson hits the big 4-0. He was in a relationship with Veda for thirteen years. They got married after seven years of dating, a small ceremony at her family's farm. He had a strange feeling the night before that he was supposed to feel more excited. He'd brushed it off as nerves. By year twelve it felt like he was married to his sister or a roommate. He misses her, though. Enough to have driven past the old apartment several times the week before. They broke up last month and this is the first new person he's slept with since his midtwenties. Ever since they broke up, he's been really understanding the value of having a familial girlfriend, someone who loves all of you, probably hates a lot of things too, but the point is, you both stay. Loyalty. Like family. Why did he give that up?

Maybe for this reason, this wild girl right here. She knows what she's doing and if he weren't drunk, he'd be so shy. His room is still full of unpacked boxes; his apartment is an embarrassing new-bachelor-type place, nothing that screams success. He takes a breath, looks up at her, thinks, *Am I doing it right?* Her eyes are closed. Maybe? *Oh my god, she's so hot;* it's actually confusing him, that she picked *him* up. He's not handsome. He is tall. That's one thing he has going for him, maybe? Despite how he feels looking at his naked body, he's not repugnant. Just completely unremark-able. People always forget his name. It didn't use to bother him until he realized he had to get back out and start dating again. He can make people laugh, he likes to read, he can fix a car, he's got a master's degree, so he leans into those qualities. But he didn't have to try at all tonight, which was good, because he doesn't know how to anymore. She was just beside him, all of a sudden, and then they played poker and she won all of his money. She said, *The least I could do is let you make out with me, after taking all your cash.* And here he is with his face in her pussy. Veda didn't like it much. He's missed it. Thirteen years with barely any pussy eating and when you get to do it, it's like winning the lottery. Veda could only come if you were basically mashing her clit hard with the palm of your hand, but this girl, she's telling him softer, softer, and he goes soft, as soft as he can, and it starts working. He can hear her breath quicken. He is finally doing something right.

Breaking up with Veda was the right idea. If he hadn't eventu-ally called it off he wouldn't have this hot girl coming in his mouth right now, screaming her head off in a way that makes him worried his neighbour is going to call the cops.

Then she says, *Fuck me, Daddy, now.*

Just like in a porn.

I don't know if anyone has ever called you Daddy in this context, but nothing anyone has ever said has ever made Gibson harder.

When he wakes up a few hours later, his mouth tastes like keys, his head is a half-blown-out speaker with the bass levels turned up, and she's pulling on her underwear in a stream of morning light, bits of dust hovering around her. She catches his eye while pulling her hair up into a ponytail. The clock says 7:45 A.M. She doesn't seem to mind that she's basically naked in front of an open window. She moves toward him. He hopes she won't kiss him because he can only imagine what his breath smells like. But she leans over him and he stops caring, he closes his eyes but then he realizes she's just grabbing her one-piece romper from where it was resting on the pillow behind his head. His face feels like a stove element on the hottest setting.

"Can I make you breakfast, or coffee?" he offers, sitting up, rubbing his face. He hopes he doesn't look as bad as he feels. In the bright, sober light of day, is she cursing her decision? Was she too drunk to sleep with? Oh my god, he hadn't considered that.

"Are you okay?" he asks, like a moron. An ugly, sweaty, bad-breathed moron. He doesn't even know if he could find more than one coffee mug. Every night he just stares at the boxes containing his things, then watches TV and falls asleep, avoiding them. He's mostly been buying coffee from the gas station across the street. But she still smiles at him, sits on the edge of the bed, runs her hand through his hair. Somehow she smells like peaches, not sweat, not hangover.

"You're so sweet," she says. "I'd really like to see you again."

He tries to look cool about it, but he's so excited he gets hard. With Veda he hadn't been able to in months. What is happening to his body? He tries to conceal it with the sheet. Who is this incredible woman? He hands her his phone.

"Put your number in here, I'd love to see you, too. Take you on a proper date." He laughs. "I don't do this. I'm not a one-night-stand kind of guy."

"You said that a lot last night," she says. "It's fate that we met, maybe? I just broke up with someone, you just broke up with someone. We're still living together, have to sort that out. But I'm a bit scared of him. He did *not* want to break up."

"Is he an asshole? Do you need me to come with you?"

"He is an asshole, yes. But I'll be fine. I'm a tough girl. I have three brothers, so I learned how to fight."

"I thought you had a sister?"

"Yeah, and a sister. I mean, *had* a sister."

"Oh fuck, sorry."

"It's okay, still getting used to it. But anyway, like I said, I know how to fight if I have to."

"Well, you shouldn't have to fight. I'll come with you. Believe me. After a breakup is when violent men get extremely violent; my sister is a social worker in a women's shelter, so I know what I'm talking about."

"You are so sweet," she says for the second time, which makes him wonder if *sweet* is a euphemism for *dull*, but then she kisses him, long and hard. "I'll let you know if I need backup. We're actually still deciding which one of us is keeping the place. But I'm not going there now, I'm actually—" She looks at the time, takes a deep breath like she's considering whether she should tell

him something. She stands up again, still only wearing her underwear, holding her red romper in her hands. "Can I trust you with
something?"

"Of course," he says. His desire debases him, as she pulls the
sides of her panties up above her hips, thumbs through the elastic.
He feels himself become dumber, devoted. He would murder her
ex-boyfriend for her. He would sell all of his belongings. He's hers.
Entirely.

"I have my final radiation treatment today. I have kidney cancer,
well, actually, I *had* kidney cancer. My screens look good, so I'm
almost one hundred percent sure I'll soon be cancer-free." She
picks up her phone and starts texting, then looks at him sideways,
like she'd told him she was late for work. He stares at the fraying
elastic on the waistband of her underwear and tries to think of
something valuable to say.

"Holy shit. Wow. But you're so vibrant." Literally nothing could
come out of his mouth right now that would be the right thing to
say, so he just babbles. "I hope I wasn't too rough on you last
night."

Jesus, no wonder she's so free, so confident. She's living for *the
day*. He considers her face, her body, her spirit as though she is
now a different person. Her resilience, her toughness, it all makes
sense now.

"Oh, don't worry about me," she says. "I like it rough."

He gets up and goes down the hall, brushing his right side
against the wall of boxes and wishing they could unpack themselves. He sorts through the sink to rinse out his one cup. She
follows, her romper and bra both now slung casually over one
shoulder. He offers her water. She watches him do this, a bemused
look on her face, which is still somehow beautiful even streaked
with last night's mascara. He tries not to stare at her breasts.

"Would you like me to drive you to the hospital? Pick you up after? Do you need anything? My love language is acts of service, you know. I like to be needed." Why is he still talking?

"Oh man, I shouldn't have said anything, you're getting weird!"

"No, no, I'm not," but he is. "Okay, sorry, I just don't know what to say. I just met you, but we felt so close last night, and I just want to be helpful. It must be so rough."

"It was no picnic, it's true," she says, looking out the glass door that leads to his back deck and then gulping down the water. She turns the cup over and drops some of the remaining water onto her hand and then rubs her face.

"Want to shower? And honestly, I'm happy to drive you to the hospital, it's no problem at all." She doesn't look like a sick person. But maybe that's not something you're supposed to say?

"It's been important to me to face this journey alone. I like to go alone to my appointments," she says, handing him back the empty cup.

"Why?"

"My ex wasn't supportive. He was so selfish. Would yell at me if I couldn't do things around the house when I was tired after treatment. So now I just want to be independent, and really take care of myself, you know?" As she talks she pulls the romper on but stops short of pulling up the top.

"Absolutely. I get that. I don't mean that to sound condescending, I just admire your strength is all." He is trying very hard to look at her face.

"Don't treat me like a cancer patient," she says. "If you take me on a good date, you still have to pound me like I'm not sick, because hopefully, I won't be!" She pulls on her bra, a lacy maroon thing that does something to Gibson's brain to make all the words he knows scramble together. He follows her back into the bedroom, where she picks up his deodorant from the nightstand, swipes it on, then smells herself. "I want to smell like you all day and get turned on by it," she says.

He puts on a shirt and they stand for a moment staring at each other awkwardly. He's aware that this might be the last time he sees her. He leads her toward the door, offering coffee, breakfast, more water, which she declines. She kisses him goodbye and as she's halfway down the walkway he calls after her.

"Hey, how old are you?"

She laughs.

"Fourteen."

"Fuck off!"

"Twenty-nine, baby. Deep in my Saturn return!"

He doesn't know what that means, so he just nods. He watches her cross the street, heading toward the subway.

He thinks about when he was twenty-nine, when he and Veda shared a one-bedroom in a triplex. He was very confident, hadn't yet developed the prominent wrinkle on his brow from walking around furrowing with anxiety. They had a dream list written on a green chalkboard in their kitchen. One of the families in the building had put it out on the stoop to give away, and Veda brought it inside and hung it from a single nail. She wrote DREAM LIST in lime bubble letters. On top was VEDA'S NOVEL. And below was GIBSON'S M.A., and then COTTAGE. Veda drew little sketches of foxes and rabbits around the word cottage. Veda cared much more about her novel than Gibson cared about his master's degree, so it's ironic that he accomplished his goal but she never did. In smaller letters on the next line was BABY with a ? And sometimes Veda would erase the ? and insert a ! Then Gibson would add !!!!! They had more practical dreams listed underneath, like a better apartment, real hardwood floors, a place with no shared walls, a washing machine. They lived near the University of Toronto in the kind of building you could walk by a hundred times and never really notice anything remarkable about it. The parquet flooring was uneven and sloping from years of student tenant wear and tear and landlord neglect. The radiators complained in clanking sounds, loudest at three in the morning. The one item on the list that they crossed off while living there was *REAL COUCH*. They'd been using the lumpy futon Veda's mother had bought her the day she left for college. They dumped it on the curb outside and debated lighting it on fire for ceremonial purposes. Instead they went back inside to take photos of the new couch for Facebook, then in its infancy, when people posted literally everything that happened in a day. They shared an account named VedaAndGibson. Their profile photo was of the dog. They had one desktop computer on a rickety desk in the corner of the living room. It was white when new but was by then a dirty oatmeal colour, with fingerprint stains on the side, sweat marks on the most-often-used keys, and stickers from bands they liked around the perimeter. On the rickety dot matrix printer they usually kicked a few times by accident whenever they sat at the desk for more than a few minutes, Veda printed drafts of her novels, and Gibson printed his papers. They called the printer Eugene. He can't remember why.

The list got ridiculous at the end of it, with things like hangoverless beer and a pet murder robot and perfect angel skin and all bosses dead! Their first Christmas living together, they decided to stay in the city and have an autonomous adult holiday away from their families. Veda's parents lived in Ottawa, and his in Owen Sound, both easy enough to get to, but they were both working second jobs in holiday retail and couldn't imagine using their one day off to travel before having to deal with Boxing Day madness. Gibson stood in line for fifty minutes at the LCBO to buy bottles of peppermint schnapps and chocolate vodka and they did snowball shooters and ate Stove Top stuffing and rotisserie chicken from the Dominion grocery store. On her way home from her shift at the Chapters bookstore in Yorkdale, Veda bought discount Christmas chocolate at Shoppers Drug Mart and they brought their mattress out to the living room to lie on "bed island" and watched *Elf*, slips of After Eight mints on their tongues. They got a bit drunk and had sex. To be having sex on Christmas in their own adult apartment and not sitting in their childhood bedrooms surrounded by their mother's sewing projects or gym equipment felt extra indulgent. In the morning they called their families and felt briefly guilty while on the phone and then, once they hung up, they got right back into the joy of having a day off where they could sleep off their sticky sweet hangovers and eat leftover chicken with 7-Eleven ramen noodles. They gave each other one present each, and were surprised to learn they had both made photo albums celebrating their year in the apartment together. Gibson still has his in the moving box he'd labelled *Important Memories*.

That February, on Veda's twenty-ninth birthday, she told him she was pregnant. He was standing at the concession stand of the Bloor rep theatre with two overflowing bags of popcorn and a bag of red licorice, excited to watch a showing of their favourite '80s comedy film, *Real Genius*. He knew something was wrong when she walked in the door a few minutes late; she used to love to settle in and watch previews. Instead she showed him the pregnancy test and said, "You go get our seats, I'm going to go pee on this." Sometimes Veda used to blurt things out that way, without any preamble. Of course he didn't go get their seats. He joined her in the bathroom, and sat on the floor, while Annex ladies told him he had to leave but he didn't move. He sat there in his oversized parka and said, "My girlfriend is in that stall and it's important I'm here for moral support." One of the ladies said he was a nice sensitive boy and that his girlfriend was lucky.

It threw their life into chaos for a while, having to do things out of order—planning to support a kid before they had any savings, before he got promoted. But after the shock of it wore off, Gibson felt like he'd become a man in a matter of weeks. He was almost thirty, after all. He did strange things during those first few weeks of preparing to be a dad—bought proper ice cube trays, researched multivitamins and child development, and talked to men in the dog park about the importance of getting on daycare lists even before the second trimester. They planned their wedding, decided to do it when the baby was a toddler. Their life would be chaos then anyway, right? By the time she miscarried, he wasn't nervous anymore, he was excited. He didn't tell her that. He said things like *We weren't ready anyway* and *We can't even keep the aloe plants alive* and *Think of how jealous Hank would be about a baby when he's our baby* and they were both sad for what felt like forever. The actual miscarriage was so physically painful and emotionally scarring for Veda that she went back on the pill and said, *When the novel is done, we'll try again.* Gibson wanted to try again right away, but he didn't say so.

The biggest fight they ever had, bigger than any spat during the divorce, was the one on the projected due date. Gibson hadn't written it down, didn't realize when it was. But Veda had quietly been tracking week to week how the baby would have developed beyond the eleven weeks. She'd mentioned it once that summer, in passing while they were camping in Algonquin Park. Something like *In November, we should have a little ceremony or do something to mark the day.* And he'd agreed. And then on the day he'd invited Julian over to play video games and when Veda got home from work, she was carrying a bunch of flowers and looking odd but not so odd that Gibson thought he should say anything beyond *You good, babe?* as he barely looked up from the screen.

He still feels bad about it. He bought a candle the next year and made her dinner. He remembered every year after that to at least say something. Eventually, they decided to try again, and for the following few months they became obsessed with it. But after three months without success, Veda said she didn't want to anymore. She said they would try again after she finished the book. When she'd said that, Gibson remembers thinking, *But what if you never do?* But he couldn't verbalize that without sounding like he didn't believe in her. He doesn't quite know what happened in the intervening years. Suddenly he was thirty-nine and single again. They never got pregnant again. A few years ago, they just stopped having sex. They still cuddled at night and held hands while walking, but it was as though the idea of sex didn't even occur to them. At least not with each other. Sometimes they'd have a date night and end up having the kind of sex that was perfunctory and absent of intimacy, but those dates got farther and farther apart.

He wonders if Veda is having sex with someone new now. He still remembers everything about Veda's body, the birthmark between her breasts shaped like Alaska, her strangely shaped pinky toe, how impossibly soft her skin was. He remembers the black Converse sneakers and jean skirt she wore on their first date. He remembers the things that he could say, in the right circumstances, that would drive her wild. Have they changed? Are turn-ons fixed or do they change with every lover? He's still staring out at the street, the too-bright day making him squint, when he gets a text message from Cammie. A photo of her boobs pops up with her number. *I like you,* it says. His grin fills the whole apartment. Thoughts of Veda disintegrate. He contemplates licking the screen. It's like his body is back online. Yesterday he'd been planning to try to woo Veda back, but now the idea of going back to her seems crazy. He gets a swirl of nausea and runs to the bathroom. He's known Cammie for less than twenty-four hours, but he is the kind of happy no man should be when he's gripping the toilet after dry heaving from a hangover. But he is. He's truly, authentically happy for the first time in over a year. An ebullient, frantic joy in his chest, even as he leans his pounding head against the cool toilet seat and sends a text to Julian that reads *Glad you had a good birthday but no shots ever again in this one precious life.*

2

Shelby's doctor leaves her a voicemail in a breezy tone that says *Please call back to discuss the lab results.* This fills Shelby with terror but not urgency. Instead of rushing to reply, she avoids it. Shelby has two speeds: frantic or a dulled and gauzy paralysis. She can't handle any more bad news right now. She sinks into her apricot linen sheets. They smell faunal from neglect. Her alarm goes off, the one she labelled before she went to bed with *YOU WILL LEAVE THE HOUSE TODAY.*

Shelby lives in a semidetached three-storey Victorian on Palmerston Boulevard. It once belonged to her parents and is now hers alone. She has lived in Toronto her whole life, except for the four years she attended Trent University in Peterborough, where she technically majored in cultural studies but excelled mostly at having afternoon tea and sex dates with women who wore purple overalls. Most people walking by Shelby's house remark on the loveliness of the mint-green porch against the ivory brick, the soft raw-wood shutters, and the bright block of cedar hedges. Shelby's wife, Kate, made the new exterior and landscaping her final home improvement project before she died.

Shelby has only ventured beyond the porch a handful of times in the previous weeks. The last time she left, she walked to the corner store to buy toilet paper and rhubarb seltzer. She was feeling quite satisfied about this accomplishment, but then she ran into Sabrina, the grey-haired tarot card reader from the brick house across the street. Her husband, a bedraggled professor of labour rights, waved from the porch. He wears his hair in a long grey ponytail. When Kate nicknamed him Mr. Ponytail, Shelby immediately forgot his real name. She had never thanked them for the boxes of muffins they'd dropped off following Kate's death. So when Sabrina approached her on the sidewalk, forcing a sandalwood-stinking hug, Shelby said, "It's weird to think her brain just blew up, you know? It could happen to any of us!" Her voice had come out pitchy and high, an indicator that she was not being herself. She has a normal tone of voice that comes out automatically when she is comfortable with someone. This pitch meant she was overwhelmed. Sabrina nodded her head and whispered her condolences. After that, Shelby vowed to only use the back door and the side alleyway from then on.

But today she's going to make breakfast and then leave the house. She wants to keep her promise to Olive, the one friend who stuck around after Kate's funeral, who said, "Promise me you'll try the grief support group. Just once." At the time, Shelby had nodded yes, but today she has a feeling in her neck. A swollen gland? She googles "lymph node cancer" while pacing the black-and-white-tiled kitchen floor, scrolling and trying to sip water even though swallowing feels impossible. When she looks up "difficult to swallow," the results show a list of terrible reasons, the most obvious being anxiety. But she doesn't believe anxiety is ever the cause of anything, only the result of the thing she fears the most.

Shelby has had health anxiety for as long as she can remember. She remembers worrying about cancer and AIDS as far back as grade one. Her body was always telling her that something was off. She had an acute sensitivity to the smallest shifts, an inability to stop thinking about those shifts. If she scratched her arm she would stare at it constantly, waiting for the signs of blood poisoning or cat scratch fever.

But she also knew from a young age that she shouldn't talk about her distress with anyone. She started doing compulsions to ward off the bad luck of it all. She crossed her fingers for good luck for the whole year when she was eight, and her fingers grew crooked; you can see the way they curl even now, in her thirties.

She forces herself to select an egg from the carton in the fridge and place it in a small copper saucepan and fill it with water. She makes sure the egg sinks, because that means it hasn't gone bad. She turns the burner on high and goes back to scrolling every symptom of throat cancer.

The ironic thing about this new surge of health anxiety is that the only other emotional state Shelby finds herself in is suicidal ideation, a lower type of low than she's ever experienced, leaving her incapable of even the simplest physical ability. She will lie on the couch not just unmotivated but basically incapable of the necessary movements of life, rising only to care for her dog. When this state goes on for too long she gets freaked out and falls prey to anxiety again.

Kate was the best at reassurance. If she were here right now she would say, *Let's call the doctor together. I'll dial and you just have to do the talking. It's probably nothing big.* She would listen to whatever anxiety Shelby was experiencing and she'd say, *I'm here. You're safe. And if you need to, we'll go to the doctor. But what if you tried to just take five deep breaths and distract yourself for a few minutes and then see if you feel the same way?* But now Shelby is alone, without Kate's soothing instructions. Everywhere she looks she sees danger.

Every feeling in her body spells out the end. She turns the stove element off and goes back to her bedroom. She sits on the edge of the bed with one hand absently tracing her dog's neck.

She wakes up every day and her first thought is that she is alive and Kate isn't, and that thought makes all the sensations of being alive, the banality and wonder of inhaling and exhaling without effort, seem like a joke. But her anxiety about her health comes rushing back to interrupt her grief-fuelled lethargy. She doesn't want to die unless she's in charge of deciding the departure time.

A primary experience of hypochondria involves the wish to share one's body, to ask *Do you feel this too?* There's a crushing unreliability when you're the only person who knows that something feels off. You either fear doctors or don't trust that they are ever thorough enough. It's not like when you taste something funny, and you can pass a forkful across the table and ask *Does this also taste off to you?* This feeling of a lump in the throat, a burning of the tongue, a scratch where there should be softness, a pain where there should be none. It's enough to drive you mad, that no one can verify what you're feeling except you. The extra sensitivity to every sensation in your body makes you an unreliable narrator of your own experience. Most partners before Kate became annoyed with Shelby. Her anxiety was too much. They ended up taking on a parental role, and it was never sexy.

She did years of therapy—first cognitive behavioural with a mousy brunette named Holly at the clinic on Dupont Street, where she left her shoes on the jute rug at the door and scanned the books in the waiting room. *Mists of Avalon? Puppy Training 101? C. S. Lewis?* She judged it all. CBT was expensive and self-congratulatory in tone, and the results were up and down. Then talk therapy, which was comforting but yielded fewer results, and she couldn't stop the inner monologue that she was boring the therapist. She heard herself composing the narrative of Shelby's Life Story and could not stop questioning it—what was the truth? Then medication—Zoloft made the biggest dent in her anxiety game. The combination of all three meant she was improving, able to live in the present, but occasionally she woke up and it was back in full force, and it felt like all the therapeutic mitigation had been for naught. But her life became much more manageable thanks in part to the support of Kate, who had both endless patience and an understanding of disordered anxiety herself. When they found each other they felt uniquely able to care for the parts of the other that had driven their previous partners crazy.

Ever since Kate died, Shelby has felt everything acutely again. A comprehensive list of her fears would be an entire book unto itself, but here is an abbreviated selection: blood clots, strokes, one-eye blindness (slow), both-eyes blindness (sudden), melanoma, cat scratch fever, botulism, meningitis, endless vertigo, the disease where your runny nose is actually leaking brain fluid, the flesh-eating disease, suddenly losing her memory while away from her house, fainting, head injuries that result in sudden impulsiveness or a loss of empathy, shouting out rude or offensive things, dropping a baby, going crazy and hitting a frail person or senior citizen, driving over a bridge and impulsively driving off the side to her death. You get the idea.

It's ironic that the one of them who wasn't afraid of death was the one to go down suddenly and finally. Kate was a vegan. She didn't smoke or drink. She jogged five days a week. She'd done drugs when she was younger but she'd been sober five years. And yet she's gone. She will never exist again, as the four-year-old standing on a chair eating a whole jar of sauerkraut while her mother's back was turned, or as the thirty-one-year-old on the roller coaster with her nephew while Shelby stood on the ground taking photos of their windswept faces.

She wore Kate's favourite plaid shirt, navy and robin's egg blue, to work every day for two weeks before HR told her she should take a bereavement break. Before the incident in the elevator, and the ambulance, and all the pills. Shelby worked as an administrator at the local culinary college, a position she took as a summer gig after university that she never left. She kept getting raises and title changes, and eventually her benefits package was too good to give up, especially since she didn't know what else to do with her life.

It's been ten minutes and Shelby is still worried about this feeling in her throat. She should call the doctor back. She takes her temperature with the thermometer she keeps in the bedside table: 98.24, perfect. It gives her five minutes of calm. She used to carry a thermometer in her purse and take her temperature every time she felt anxious. She'd stopped the compulsion for the last year or two, and has recently started again. She ordered a fancy one that cost ninety dollars from Amazon, along with several cheaper ones from the drugstore so she'd have one for her backpack, her purse, her bathroom. She always wants to be able to reach out and get a read on her internal well-being.

It's been three months. Her friends are exhausted. *You don't seem to be getting better,* they say. *It's hard to know what to do.* Olive said that, clearly exasperated. *You're not eating. I bring food and it spoils. I'm worried. She died, you didn't. You need to live!* Shelby had never wanted to punch anyone as much as she wanted to punch Olive, standing in her foyer in ugly aquamarine workout shorts. That *RIP Aaliyah* T-shirt she wears, even though she's the whitest girl on earth. Her ironic silver fanny pack. And the fucking herbal tinctures. So many left on Shelby's bathroom sink. One fell and broke, and now the bathroom smells like a witch's brew, haunted and like a forest and also like rot, like death. Her mother brings flowers, she does her dishes, collects the mail.

Shelby stands up shakily and keeps her phone in her hand just in case she faints and hits her head and has to call 911 from the ground. She walks back to the kitchen and stands at the island, paws at the bag of bread, noting it has gone mouldy before she's had more than one slice. Buying food when you live alone is a race to eat things before they spoil. She never wins the race. Trying to eat when you can't even remember what it feels like to be hungry is like trying to force yourself to drink when you're already drowning. Every day Shelby manages a cup of coffee, half a smoothie with spinach, yogurt, protein powder, and strawberries, maybe a handful of cashews, a few bites of whatever her mom drops off. She keeps cashews in a teacup beside the dish rack and tries to eat one now. She knows she's lost weight because people keep telling her she looks good. The last time someone told her—her aunt, who was dropping off food—she didn't say thank you, only grimaced. Why are people complimenting her visible pain? When Shelby is happy and calm she is not thin. Only Kate understood that.

"I don't know what's wrong with her," Shelby heard her mother say to her father on the phone. "Why can't she get over the fact that her friend died?"

Kate wasn't her friend, she was her wife, her partner of six years. Her mother still can't say *girlfriend*, let alone *wife*. Shelby told her to get out, not to come back. She didn't need her. She wouldn't understand. But then she came back around with groceries and they acted like it didn't happen and it was better than having no one in the room with her sometimes, breathing the same air, relating to her as a fellow alive person.

How can you just have an aneurysm and die, two seconds and you're gone? Kate was standing in HomeSense, buying a new bed for the dog. She loved the dog. Coach Taylor is the only reason Shelby has gone outside in almost a week. He's the reason she keeps going, if she's honest. If Coach were to die too, she'd probably wander down to the lake with rocks in her pocket like Virginia.

Shelby swallows the cashews and attempts a shower. An oily swirl of orange and white peach shampoo, under the hot water, briefly sends her away from herself. The feeling of her fingertips against the green tile, for thirty seconds she is okay. Perhaps not okay, but neutral. And then she looks at the tile and remembers how proud she'd been when Kate had installed the tile herself and it was perfectly symmetrical, and Shelby had kissed her on the mouth when she saw it, and said, *You're perfect, the perfect wife.* She'd led her away from the bathroom and onto the living room couch and gone down on her. She moans at the memory. It's crazy to think she'll never be able to do that again. Shelby didn't tell Kate the chemicals from the tile glue gave her a headache, and that she woke up at two A.M. and googled "headaches from chemical smells + poisoning."

———

The grief group is held at the Jewish Community Centre at Bloor and Spadina, only a few blocks away from her house. She gives herself plenty of time but gets halfway down the walk before she notices the way her body feels different, which makes her heart start up its manic drum solo before she remembers she's just not wearing a bra. These are the kinds of things that cause her alarm: any slight variation in embodiment. When she goes back inside, the dog thinks she's back and gets so excited he tips over the water bowl. Shelby pulls her sports bra out of her gym bag, long abandoned, and puts it on even though it gives her uniboob. She refills the water bowl. Then she realizes she'd left the movie *Carol* on the TV, the movie she's watched every weekend for weeks. She digs around for the remote behind the couch cushions. She is grossed out by the tapestry of crumbs she can feel and gives up, leaving it on for Coach Taylor. When she locks the door a second time, she longs to be back inside, braless and spooning the dog, watching the movie she's memorized, where she always knows what's going to happen. But longing to be on the couch feels better than being on the couch.

She doesn't play out the scene as she'd imagined it the night before. She'd pictured a leisurely walk, getting a coffee on Harbord before heading north. Instead it's a warm afternoon. The sidewalks are jammed with people. She walks fast, arrives sweaty.

She gets in the elevator and presses 3 with her elbow several times, not quite hitting the sensor properly until the third try. The floor is sticky with spilled drink, or at least she hopes that's what it is, so she crams into the back corner. She points to the spill when a man gets on at the second floor, but he ignores her. The ride is jumpy, the elevator making disconcerting metal-on-metal sounds, and she's relieved when the heavy doors part haltingly on her desired floor. She walks slowly down the hall, looking at the numbers on the doors, half hoping she'll get lost and have an excuse to go home. But she finds it, a fairly large classroom with a row of windows on one side, the sun beaming into her eyes, illuminating a rainfall of dust. She is last to arrive. She doesn't care, though— one gift of grief is that she barely cares about any social convention anymore. The group is seated in a circle. There's a snack table by the door—store-bought cookies in the shape of maple leaves that Shelby last ate in preschool, squares of toothpicked orange cheddar cheese, rows of Ritz crackers, cupcakes with gummy worms on the icing. Shelby would have been excited to eat these things months ago, but now they look like plastic facsimiles of food. She writes her name in purple marker on a *HELLO MY NAME IS* tag and sticks it across the coffee stain on the breast of her plaid cotton dress, the only semiclean thing in the house.

"Welcome, everyone," says a woman with a thick bob of processed reddish-orange hair, a line of grey roots delineating a haphazard middle part.

Group members murmur. No one looks devastated; these could all be strangers on a bus and she'd never know they were grieving. Shelby looks up at the clock. An hour seems interminable. A woman who is knitting a lavender scarf while she talks says she's started a gratitude journal. Oh shit. This isn't the right group for her. What the fuck does she have to be grateful for? She doesn't need people to tell her to be grateful or offer platitudes that can be sewn into throw pillows sold at HomeSense, she needs people who know what it's like to want to be as dead as the person they're grieving. She requires spit and blood and desperation, not embroidery or any gloss over real feeling. Shelby is trapped on a bad group date she can't get out of when Cammie walks into the room. Only she doesn't yet know she's Cammie, doesn't know her life is about to be divided into Before Cammie and After Cammie. Right now she just sees a thin brunette with blond highlights wearing a red romper and white cowboy boots, who pulls a chair from a stack in the corner and joins the group. She sits down like no one ever taught her how to sit in a chair properly, one leg propped up, the other curled under, like a weird spider. She looks too good to be in mourning, too young for this group, which looks like it could be the audition room for a menopause supplement commercial. When she sits, the light from the window frames her perfectly and she looks like an Instagram ad for the boots, or some type of life coach. Everyone looks at her, taking her in. Before she even says anything you can tell she is the star of the group. The first time Shelby hears Cammie talk, she has an uncanny feeling that she's going to know her someday. Cammie volunteers to share right away; her right knee shakes and she pulls at a thread on her shorts. A purple Gatorade bottle sticks out of her beige suede purse. She twirls a ring on her finger as she talks. "Today has been a really hard one. Next week is the one-year anniversary of Leslie's death, and my mom wants to go to the beach to discard her ashes, but Leslie hated the water. I'm so mad at her. My mom seems so remote, like she doesn't care at all."

She pauses for a moment, turns to look Shelby in the eye, and says, "You're new. I'm Camilla. Chatterbox, oversharer, main-character-syndrome-having Cammie."

"I'm Shelby," Shelby says, barely getting the words out. "General undersharer. My wife died. Now I can't taste anything."

Cammie laughs. Shelby hasn't made anyone laugh in a very long time. "I remember that phase of it," she says. Shelby laughs at this, though it's not funny, but the laugh is more an utterance of relief, that she is in a phase that will change and maybe even end; she won't always be here.

Cammie jumps back into her monologue. Shelby is rapt as she brings the group alive, like an orchestra conductor. She can see it in their faces; these older women react to Cammie like she's a handsome young boy, almost flirtatiously. Cammie acknowledges them all, somehow, managing to bring things they've said in previous weeks into her share.

Shelby wasn't sure she wanted to say anything to the group, but she needn't have worried. Cammie takes the reins and keeps on going. Everything she says about grief puts into words these deeply physical sensations Shelby has been experiencing. After the group is over, Shelby lingers by the snack table, pretending to look for something in her purse. She tries to think of something to say to Cammie and comes up with nothing. Eventually she finds the washroom, and when she exits a stall Cammie is standing at the sink applying bright-red lipstick.

"I'm so happy to see someone under forty, you have no idea," she says, smacking her lips together and holding eye contact with Shelby in the mirror.

"You said so many things I could relate to," Shelby says, running her hands under a weak stream of tap water.

"Want to grab an iced coffee downstairs?" Cammie asks.

Even though Shelby half wants to run back home to her safe spot on the couch, she nods.

———————

They sit across from each other at the Second Cup. An old man at the adjacent table is falling asleep into his hands. Packs of teenagers shout as they walk by outside. Shelby picks at a pumpkin muffin as she listens to Camilla's entire story from birth to present day. It is like a horror movie, her life, and by comparison, the loss of Kate suddenly seems like a walk in the park. Cammie discovered her sister when she died by suicide. They'd had a fight the night before. Her sister was an addict. Cammie had taken out a line of credit to pay for her rehab three times. She thought it would finally stick and it didn't. Her father had also killed himself, exactly ten years before her sister did. There is so much sorrow in her story, yet she is able to crack jokes.

"I'm a suicide magnet," she says. "My best friend also offed herself. Her name was Morgan."

"I don't know what to say to that, except I'm sorry."

"You don't need to know what to say," she says, kindly. "It's fucked up! There's no language for it that makes sense."

They exchange numbers.

"Text me anytime. Anytime you feel like you're drowning. I get it. I'll always respond," Cammie says as she's crumpling up her napkin and taking the final sips of a mocha latte.

"Me too," Shelby offers.

"No, it's too early for you. You just use me. I've got other people to lean on. I can tell you're not ready to be there for anyone else yet. I won't ask anything from you. Believe me, I wish I'd had someone like that for me when my sister died."

It was such a kind observation, so considerate. They exit the coffee shop. Bloor Street is filled with rush-hour walkers. *The world just keeps going,* Shelby thinks, watching them push by her, harried and troubled by the wind and traffic. Cammie stands still, obstructing the commuters' path, and doesn't seem to hear them sigh and huff to get around her.

"Tell anyone who thinks you should be better already to fuck off. Take a nap for a week, or for a month if you fucking need to. Fuck them for thinking they know what's good for you. They don't know. God willing, they never will," she says.

As Cammie is speaking, Shelby thinks about how maybe it's true, that God or the universe or whoever does provide you with the people you need when you most need them. Cammie feels like a radical intervention in the dreary sleepwalking life Shelby has sustained since Kate's death.

"Going to the subway?"

"No," Shelby says, "I live nearby."

Cammie hugs her and starts west on Bloor. Shelby watches her head toward the subway doors before she turns south on Spadina, feeling almost like a human being again. She stops at the flower market on Harbord and buys sunflowers, Kate's favourite, and a peach, a cucumber, a lime, a fistful of fresh mint, a block of feta cheese. Standing in line she has a horrifying thought—does she have a crush? No. Cammie isn't physically her type. She is too feminine, too young. She pictures her lips, and she decides that she definitely doesn't want to kiss her. Shelby is the only one of her friends who never falls for straight girls. She likes women who look like John Goodman or Pete Davidson, skater boys or baseball prodigies. People used to think Kate was her son, which was both creepy and hilarious. But what is this feeling? She clutches the white plastic bag so hard it makes dents in her palm as she walks west on Harbord and crosses Bathurst. When she gets home, the dog is waiting, betrayed by how long she's left him alone. She gives him treats, a whole palmful, and lets him sit on the tall stool beside her while she makes a salad, like he's a little dog sous chef. She takes a bite to see if it might need more salt or lime, and her taste buds come back online. The brine of the feta, the citrus sparkle, the crunch. She can detect it all.

She gives Coach Taylor his afternoon medicine, two pills inside treats, and lets him run around in the backyard while she eats. He doesn't really run so much as amble around like a bunny, sniffing the ground and then picking a spot on the grass to lie in the sun. She pulls out one of the patio chairs, fishing the cushions that she hadn't bothered to take out this summer out of the plastic bench they hide in during the winter. She puts her feet up on the oversized planter that used to house a geranium she neglected to death. She finishes the entire bowl. She scrapes at the herbs and oil, pressing a stray parsley leaf with her finger and eating it. Putting the bowl down on the ground, she realizes it's the only thing she's finished in weeks. She puts "Grief Group" as a Wednesday reminder in her phone and genuinely looks forward to the next one. Just seven days to get through until then. She stares at Coach Taylor, now alert enough to be gleefully stalking a squirrel, and she's able to unfocus her eyes and just get lost in a daze. Moments of utter relaxation are so rare for Shelby in general, especially now.

Her phone buzzes. The doctor again. She answers, now suddenly fearful of the news to come. "Your iron levels are very low," she says. Shelby feels relief at this. She promises to buy iron supplements and hangs up. As soon as Shelby knows the source of any health problems, she stops being afraid of them. It's the unknown that is truly frightening.

When she gets up, calling Coach to the door, instead of sitting on the couch and turning on whatever TV program happens to be on, she strips the sheets from her bed and clutches them in her arms down the basement stairs to throw in the wash. Inside the washing machine is a small load of towels she'd washed the week before but had forgotten to dry, so she just adds the bedding and washes it all over again. She has not changed the sheets since Kate died. She keeps the case from Kate's pillow on, despite it turning a bit yellow from lack of washing. She can still smell Kate's hair product on it. When it started to get faint, she took the pomade from her bedside table and rubbed a finger's worth over the pillowcase.

She leans against the washing machine, feeling briefly upset that she's finally done it, but forces herself upstairs and onto the bare mattress, where she looks at her gym's website on her phone for their yoga and swim lesson schedule. She makes a breakfast date with Olive for Sunday.

3

After Gibson meets Cammie he feels as though he's living in that first five minutes after having ingested some kind of drug that makes his heart race, his thoughts definitive, colours more crisp and clear. The world around him looks different, the edges are softer. He's never been a drug person but he remembers doing mushrooms in grad school with Veda, how he'd never really seen a green as green as the grass in High Park that day.

Cammie helps him settle into his new apartment. She selects a bright yellow-green paint at the hardware store, far too bright for his taste but she convinces him. And indeed when he steps back and takes in the scene, Cammie up on the ladder finishing the top trim, it is the perfect colour for a fresh start. The room comes alive with each brushstroke, just like the cinematic movement of clouds above them as they lie on their backs in the park later that day, drips of Popsicles on their shirts, telling each other secrets. The clouds are better than any film he's seen in years. Every day they meet up at some point, and he supposes because she'd had such a scare, she'd faced her mortality so recently, each interaction feels as though it is pulsing with the potential for madness, glory, both chaos and certainty. They say things to each other that sound like corny rom-com dialogue, but Gibson sincerely means every word. He *doesn't* know how he ever lived without her. He feels like she's opened up an unknown world to him. Whenever they're apart he feels like he's missing a limb. He feels truly known.

The third weekend they're together they walk to get morning coffee, and then they swipe Gibson's card on some BIXI bikes and pedal to the water; Cammie rides her bike like a maniac—up one-way streets and a sliver away from streetcars, drawing awe and ire from drivers.

"You're going to be the death of me," he says to her at a stop-light. She reaches over to him, runs a finger along his waist.

"We just have this one dumb life, we have to feel as many things as possible!" she says, before pushing off ahead of him again.

When they get to the water he's out of breath but exhilarated. They lay their hoodies out on the sand and watch a group of friends play volleyball, and eventually a concert starts at the Budweiser Stage that they can hear, and Cammie knows the band and can sing every word. He buys her a bootleg shirt from a guy in a car and she acts like it's a diamond ring.

He has slept through most of his thirties, and now here is this person who seems to have come from another realm specifically to energize him, to destroy any feelings of spiritual, psychic, or sexual lethargy. He feels reborn in this dangerously new passion-first and passion-only life.

The only thing that remains the same in his life—besides work—are his weekly breakfast dates with Julian, Pete, and Stef at a diner on Roncesvalles. He can't remember when they started doing it, but it was sometime in their midthirties when they real-ized that unless they did something regularly, their friendship would go the way of most adult friendships—hanging out every six months, forever catching up. Their breakfasts had been the high-light of his week when things were bad with Veda. The diner is usually filled with old men and sometimes families, never hipsters or yuppies; they never have to wait in line. It is just cheap and good and unpretentious, which is hard to find in Toronto. It does have a side patio that borders a parking lot, where they sit today in the late-summer air.

Now he doesn't want to have to spend two hours without Cammie, but their breakfast date rule is no partners invited. The shift in his demeanour does not go unnoticed. "You're so different when you're always getting laid," remarks Julian, dousing his eggs in HP Sauce, while Stef circles his pancakes in syrup like a little kid, because at home he eats keto and this breakfast is his weekly chance for a hit of carbs. Pete nudges Gibson in the ribs.

"Give us details," Pete says.

"No, gross," Gibson says, face burning. "Not ethical!"

"Come on, you're the lone unmarried. Give us something."

They usually talk about Pete and his wife, Angela, going to couples counselling. Or the girl in his office he's obsessively in love with. Gibson can tell he's happy to not be in the spotlight this week. He eats his own pancakes fast—they are warm and delicious; food has started tasting amazing again—while wishing for time to move forward. And toward the end of the meal, trying to still his thoughts and his shaking knee, they see why he's so distracted. Cammie rides her bike up to the other side of the patio fence. She's not wearing a bra and they can all see her nipples through her thin rust-coloured T-shirt. She greets his friends, cracks a few jokes that make them laugh. The whole time she's subtly rubbing herself on the bar of her bicycle. It drives Gibson to distraction. He hands Julian a twenty for breakfast and splits, insisting on cutting through the adjacent parking lot as he walks her back to his place, pausing behind a tall pickup truck to unzip her jean shorts and drive two fingers inside her. *You were doing that for me,* he says into her neck, *touching yourself in front of my buddies like that, getting yourself ready for me.* She can't answer because she's coming all over his hand.

4

er regular Sunday breakfast date with Olive gets her up and out of the house. Sundays are the worst days. It's when everyone else spends time with their families, and from Shelby's front porch she grows maudlin at the sight of people walking together, couples holding hands, dads pulling toddlers in wagons, visual reminders of what she no longer has. If she kills herself on a Sunday afternoon it will not be a surprise. Olive is waiting for her on the patio at Aunties & Uncles when she arrives a few minutes late. She sips a black coffee before they order food, and another with her breakfast.

"How are you?" Olive asks, emphasis on the *are*, and Shelby stops her.

"I'd rather hear about your life, actually. Anything, really, to keep my mind off my own."

Olive looks relieved at this instruction in a way that makes Shelby feel a bit resentful. Olive speaks about the TV show she is about to produce, a reality show about dating. She tells funny stories about the audition process and Shelby laughs when she knows she should, but she doesn't have an authentic reaction to anything. Olive is like a TV program on in the background that Shelby isn't absorbing.

When the cheque comes the waiter asks Shelby if the food was all right, or if she would like the remains of her breakfast in a box. Shelby apologizes for not having eaten her food and accepts the box she knows she'll put in someone's garbage on the walk home.

"I'm so glad you came out," Olive says, grinning, like they're having a great time. Shelby grins back, one hand curled in a fist in her lap and the other gripping the take-out box like she might launch it into the air at any moment.

Olive offers her a ride home. She declines. "It's such a nice day for a walk," she hears herself say as a reason. She knows a panic attack is looming and she'd rather be alone if it happens, and it does, halfway down Markham Street. What does it mean that seeing her closest friend, the one who has been consistent and firm in showing her love in actions, in practical help and just physical presence, doing all the things her grief books say a good friend should be doing, makes Shelby leave brunch feeling like she's escaping a burning room? She has to sit on the edge of the sidewalk for five minutes, letting the worst of the anxiety pass. How long can a human being go without connecting to another human being? Is she going to get stress-related illnesses, the way your body deteriorates if you aren't held tight in relational proximity?

When Shelby gets home she pulls all the cleaning products out of the hall closet and attacks each room in segments. She doesn't turn on music or a podcast, she just moves around in silence. She hears her jaw crack. A broken-speaker pulse in her ear. The sound of her breath as she pushes the mop into the corner of every stair down to the basement. When the house is clean and she sits on the porch with her hand to her chest after gulping a glass of iced tea, pondering esophageal cancer, she feels everything she was escaping through movement. Maybe it has simply been a weird few days of emotional reprieve, but here she is, back to the normal crushing weight of it all. When she sees her neighbour, the professor of labour with the grey ponytail whose name she can never remember, she offers a weak wave and then stands as though she just remembered something and must go inside. At the kitchen island she pours some whiskey into the remains of her tea, gulps it down, and turns on the TV.

She wakes up around midnight when her phone buzzes with a photo of cleavage, momentarily confusing until Shelby also sees that *CAMILLA YOUR NEW BEST FRIEND FROM DEAD PEO-PLE GROUP* is calling. Who sends semi-nudes to near strangers? She gets a feeling in her chest like she has a crush, though the idea of ever loving anyone again feels impossible. But a new friend? There is a freedom in a new friend while you're grieving. There's no expectation that you'll return to who you once were; they never knew that person anyway. The expectations are low. Still, she keeps her phone facedown against her chest as it buzzes. Shelby never answers the phone. Shouldn't someone her age text first?

Camilla doesn't leave a voicemail. A text comes in: *I have a great idea. Wanna hear it?*

Shelby is surprised that Cammie assumes she is screening and not asleep at midnight like a normal thirtysomething. Perhaps she remembers Shelby's confession that she rarely sleeps for more than a couple of hours at a go.

She looks at the text. Coach is asleep on her feet, both numb. He makes a little snuffly sound as she wiggles her toes and flexes her calves to get blood flowing again. She could just not reply. Instead she types: *Yes.*

Cammie responds immediately: *Get in a cab!!!! Meet me here!!!!*

Shelby presses the link. It's a weird address in an industrial area north of the Junction.

Girl, that is far. Wtf.

Trust me. If this were a chapter in your memoir, wouldn't future you want you to go now?

Shelby sighs. She wishes she were still in her twenties, when thoughts like that were inspiring. But she types back a weak *OK*. Though her hair is a straggling mess and she can't imagine talking to an Uber driver for even five seconds, Shelby follows Cammie's commands. She pulls the plaid dress she wore the week before over her sweatpants and shoves her hair up into a bun. Cammie texts: *Wear flat shoes* as she's standing on the sidewalk, staring at the tiny black cartoon car in the app stopped at a light on Dundas. *I'm a dyke. I wear heels at Pride, and from the dresser to the bed on special occasions.* After she presses send she wonders if Cammie will get the joke. She replies with a laughing-face emoji.

Shelby has a car, but for some reason the cab instructions feel pertinent.

———

Kate and Shelby were an island. They had couple friends whom they'd occasionally rent a cottage with, or invite over for dinner, but they were a team. No one ever invited one without the other. Over the years the people who started out as their individual friends became their shared friends. After Kate died, she'd tried to go solo to Ange and Robin's house for taco Tuesday and it was so awkward, the three of them at the table. They tried really hard to make it normal, but it just couldn't be. Shelby kept going to the bathroom to deep breathe, because Ange kept blurting out weird things about Kate, like *Would you like some sour cream or do you hate it, like Kate did?* They keep inviting her, but she makes excuses. Eventually she's going to just tell them that being with them makes her feel even more alone than she feels when she's at home by herself.

This feeling she is having about Cammie is just the sparkle of a new friend, like she felt in grade school with Caroline Camper. She does need a sidekick. She listens to the Weakerthans on her phone on the ride to meet Cammie. She takes a photo of a streetlight's romantic blur on Ossington, posting it to an Instagram story. She captions it *Know the things we need to say / been said already anyway / by parallelograms of light* and turns her phone off like she's getting on an airplane. She's comforted by the white noise of the car in motion, the coolness of the windowpane against her cheek. At Hallam she sees her ex-girlfriend Rachel paused at the light on a BMX bike, doubling a woman with bright-green sneakers, her arms wrapped around her neck. They are listening to a classic Tribe Called Quest song, rapping along flawlessly, from a tiny boom box attached to Rachel's handlebars. She marvels that Rachel still looks and acts like she did at twenty-two. She stares at the tableau of them as they reach the other side of the street, wobbling and singing the chorus, and it occurs to her that her life isn't over, that it's possible to fall in love again, that her life could continue without Kate if she could only figure out how to move the boulder of grief out of her path.

5

At 7:30 A.M. Gibson and Cammie wake to the blare of tandem emergency alert texts on either side of the bed. Gibson grabs his phone and reads aloud, his voice rising in volume and higher in pitch with each word as he sits up, then stands beside the bed: " 'An incident was reported at the Pickering nuclear power plant. This is a message for those within ten kilometres of the Pickering Nuclear Generating Station. There has been NO abnormal release of radioactivity and emergency staff are responding to the situation. Remain tuned in to local media.' What the hell?" He nudges Cammie, who has fallen back asleep. Gibson googles how far he lives from the plant. Cammie groans. They aren't in the worst zone, but they aren't safe either. He gets back in bed and looks up how far one has to be to be unaffected by an incident, visions of the *Chernobyl* HBO show clicking in his head, as Cammie rolls on top of him.

"Is it the end of the world? For real?"

Does she look excited? Gibson, still scrolling for facts about what is happening, reaches over to turn on the clock radio to CBC News, but they aren't talking about it. His whole body surges with anxiety, while Cammie looks like someone just handed her a million dollars.

"Look, if it's coming for us, we better have fun while we're here!" she says, grabbing his phone and throwing it across the room. She climbs on top of Gibson, pulling his boxers down and working him with her hand while Gibson's head is half a mess of 1980s childhood terror images of nuclear demise. She puts one hand on his face and whispers, "Shhhh," even though he isn't speaking, and reaches into the nightstand for a condom. Cammie is half laughing, half moaning as she rides him, and Gibson comes quickly, just as more alerts come in. A false alarm. Gibson starts to laugh, sitting up and catching his breath as Cammie gets up to grab them glasses of water.

"You should call in sick," she suggests, gulping hers down.

"No, I never call in sick. It's like a point of pride."

"That's dumb. When you're on your deathbed are you going to wish you went to work, or stayed in bed fucking all day until it was time to eat pizza?"

"We did just narrowly avoid nuclear crisis," he says, and starts a text to his boss that he won't be in. He hems and haws over the wording for so long that Cammie grabs the phone, presses send.

———

Gibson only recently met Cammie, but he feels like he's known her for a long time. It's not just the sex. It's definitely a big part of their connection but it's not the only thing. He used to be a cynic, standing on the sidelines of life, judging and complaining. Now he gets it. He thinks about this when he drops Cammie at work at five P.M., and then picks up Julian so they can head over to the Canadian Tire on St. Clair to pick up propane and other things they need for the weekend barbecue. He pulls into a spot on Davenport. A few metres away, Julian is waiting for him on the sidewalk but is expecting him to arrive in his old Toyota Camry. He leans out the passenger-side window and calls Julian's name.

"Dude, over here!"

Julian is startled by how high the cab is, laughs as he settles in. "Are you a country singer? Did you buy some cattle?"

"I just wanted a change. I traded the car in and leased this guy. You like?"

"It's just very different, I guess," he says.

"You know Cammie is a country girl too, right? We were talking all night last weekend about wanting to get some land, build a dream home, get some goats, you know?"

"I thought you never wanted to go back to Owen Sound."

"Nah, I said I didn't want to go back there and be poor. I'd love to go back and have everything I needed, and the space, you know? The city just isn't as exciting to me anymore."

"Okay, man, sure. And Cammie wants this too? Isn't it a little early to be dreaming up the future together?"

"Maybe," he says. They watch a group of toddlers cross at Lansdowne and Davenport. Gibson turns on the radio. He rarely feels like talking to Julian is as effortful as it is now.

When Julian changes the subject with a generic "How was your day?" and Gibson confesses that he called in sick, he's embarrassed but tries not to look it. He's not sure how to explain how he feels about Cammie to Julian without sounding like he's losing his mind. He feels known. *She understands me. It's hard to explain, but it's like she can anticipate everything about what I might want, or want to talk about. She really listens.* Gibson goes on and on, all the way to the store. He emphasizes all the things they have in common— a long list, longer than anyone he's ever dated before.

When he pulls into a parking spot and cuts the ignition, Julian says, "Look, man. I'm *all* for you getting laid and having some new experiences, just be careful. She's young. You haven't been out there on the dating scene. I did it, for five years! Women are crazy. Take your time with her."

"Women are crazy? What are you, a podcaster? I'm almost forty. I wasted so much time. I don't want to do that anymore. I am ready for this love we're experiencing."

Julian raises his hands in surrender and opens the door. "I get it, man, I get it. Compatibility is a big thing."

They walk toward the doors in silence, and once in the store, Gibson mumbles that he has to pick up some things for the new apartment and he'll meet him by the cash. Gibson cools down as he wanders the kitchen aisle, thinking about how he might explain it better to Julian, this feeling that he never knew what closeness was before. He's trying to build a persuasive defence for Julian in his head. He didn't like the look of skepticism on his face, though it was better than the look of pity he's been getting since the divorce.

He picks up a stack of Tupperware and puts it in his shopping basket. An adult would have these. And some good steak knives; a man would have those. He picks the midrange price of everything. Nothing cheap, nothing too pretentious. Veda did all the shopping for this kind of stuff for years. He doesn't even really know what a kitchen needs until he tries to cook and can't find a colander or the right knife. The song "Nothing Compares 2 U" comes on the store speakers. This was the song he danced to with Felicity Cleary at the grade six graduation dance. The whole time they were dancing he kept thinking, *I can't believe someone wants to dance with* me. Somehow he had gotten to be twelve and the idea of a girl liking him was preposterous. Yet there she was, in her maroon dress and bright-pink ankle boots, leaning her head against his shoulder. Felicity was short, which he liked, because that year so many of the girls were taller than the boys. As the song came to a close she looked up at him and he realized she was expecting a kiss and so, despite feeling like he might die of fear, he placed his lips on hers for a few seconds, and then pulled away as the song changed to "Poison" by Bell Biv DeVoe and she ran back to her friends at the edge of the gym and Tom Germaine snickered *Nice one, virgin* in his ear.

He stares at the display of coffee makers. Cammie likes cappuccinos. Sometimes if he's bored at night he'll bring her one at work from Starbucks. He picks out a small espresso machine, one more stylish than he'd usually go for. She'll like it. They both grew up on instant coffee and Carnation creamer. This will impress her.

He catches up with Julian in the long checkout line. It's still awkward.

"Look, I think the best way to describe it is that I finally have what you guys have," he says. Julian and Kelly are rare among their peers in that they are still affectionate and hot for each other.

"Bro, you do not have to filibuster this. I believe you," Julian says, selecting a few packs of batteries from the impulse bin and adding them to his basket of barbecue tongs, napkins, and patio lanterns, as they wait for the woman ahead of them at the cash register to slowly and deliberately pay for six cans of cat food.

But Gibson can see and feel that he is being placated. Maybe he won't be able to explain it right now. Maybe he has to just be at peace with it.

———

The previous Sunday, Cammie had told him about how she'd had a boyfriend in Los Angeles for a while, and she'd even moved there to be with him. He was very wealthy and she never had to pay for anything, but she got a job in a Palisades coffee shop so that she would have her own money, and she served Brad Pitt a latte every morning. One time he'd invited her to his hotel. She didn't go, she said, because it was when he was married and she wasn't like that. Most people would have gone for the experience, he'd said. *Not me, I'm loyal.*

He relays this story to Julian as they push their carts toward the truck.

"I like that she's loyal, that she even uses that kind of word," he says.

Gibson sees everything in his day-to-day differently now. When he shaves he doesn't just see his drawn skin in the mirror streaked with flecks of shaving cream and dust, he remembers her hand on his cheek the night before. When he drives to work he has to be careful not to go through stoplights because his brain plays a loop of images from the night before, and it eclipses the real-life screen ahead of him. He's still distracted now, thinking about what they did all day, as he pops open the back of his truck so they can wrestle the propane tank into place.

"This truck makes me want to buy lumber and build something," says Julian.

"Ha, you don't need anything."

"Doesn't everyone need a woodshop in the backyard?"

"So you can build . . . what?"

"Right, right. I know. Your country boy daydream has me wishing for more free time, a cottage or something."

"Doesn't Kelly have a cottage?" Kelly comes from very old money.

"It's for the whole family, and it's never relaxing with everyone fighting over their time there."

"That's the dream, right? Your own getaway? I want that for me and Cammie," he says.

Julian raises his eyebrows. "Okay, okay, now you're freaking me out. I'm just going to say it. You're acting like you're in some romantic comedy. Come back to earth."

"I'm in love." He says it like *Shut up*.

"Are you going to tell Veda? I mean, I hear she's not doing great."

"I guess I'll have to. We're having lunch tomorrow. Not great how?"

"Just don't tell her yet, not until it's been a little while. I told Kelly I wouldn't tell you what Veda has been saying, but just be gentle with her."

Gibson nods, feeling guilty as he drives Julian home, mostly in silence. Kelly is sitting on the porch when they arrive, and she comes down the steep front steps to help carry things up. Kelly is wary of why he left Veda. What had been a solid couple-couple friendship has fractured somewhat. Gibson and Julian make it to the first landing and Gibson hands off his side of the tank to Kelly. He used to have a crush on her when they first met, with her big brown eyes and those impossibly long lashes, an exaggerated hourglass figure that used to make her self-conscious but she was now dressing to emphasize. Gibson doesn't want to lose Kelly's respect now that he's being open about his new love. The barbecue will be a big deal.

When he gets home, he opens Facebook and scrolls through photos from all of Julian and Kelly's barbecues from the last decade. It looks like a flip-book, watching everyone rapidly lose their hair and gain weight and get brow furrow lines and crow's-feet. At last year's barbecue he and Veda had fought over who forgot to pick up the hamburger buns, a ridiculous argument that devolved into a fight in the Loblaws parking lot about who was a more considerate person. He could see only now, with time, that the fight had really been about their exhaustion, their

inability to see the other person as the one they'd loved and cher-
ished for so long.

He sets up the new espresso maker for the morning. He
sprays the kitchen down with the vinegar and baking soda mixture Cammie made in a spray bottle from the dollar store. He
wants the apartment to look great if Cammie decides to crash
after her shift ends. When he gets into bed he almost forgets that
he has to see Veda for lunch the next day, that he took the afternoon off so he could potentially deal with the emotional impact
of said interaction.

———————

The next day is a cloudless, perfect twenty-two degrees. Gibson
sits at his desk eating a stale oatcake dipped in cold coffee, staring
out the window at the skyline over the Gardiner Expressway and
the water beyond. He can't work. He can only think about how he
will see Veda in forty-seven minutes.

For the first few years that he lived in Toronto he forgot about
the lake. It was a lake for tourists, for people who could afford to
live near it. Last summer he made a habit of riding his bike across
the bridge and down to Sunnyside Park on his lunch hour, just to
look out and away from his life. This was when things with Veda
were starting to go bad but he wasn't able to understand why he
was often feeling so peculiar. He blamed his job. He spent hours
in the evening applying for new jobs in other cities without telling
Veda what he was doing, looking for an escape hatch.

Toronto is quiet in August in Liberty Village, a once-barren and
industrial part of town south of Queen Street West that is now
home to ugly condos and mall stores and many of the country's
film and TV production offices. Most of the wealthy people leave to
work from their summer cottages, leaving just the midlevel folks

and the interns running the show. Gibson doesn't identify with his job. He could take it or leave it. It involves accounting and budgets and making sure the creative people don't go hog wild. He never thinks of work after he exits the elevator, crosses the lobby with its glut of fake potted plants and Darlene playing Candy Crush on her phone at the security desk. He's senior enough to take an afternoon off when he needs it without explanation. He gets four weeks' paid vacation. He's fine.

He pours the remainder of his coffee into the office kitchen sink and rinses his cup before forcing a spot for it in the crowded dishwasher. The smell of all the dirty dishes makes him gag but he doesn't turn it on. Tina, his boss, comes in to grab her Tupperware of salad and seeds. They banter while she pours the salad dressing. She used to call him her work husband before she got a real one and it got awkward. A few days ago she told him she was pregnant. And then in the elevator leaving work she confessed she didn't want to come back after her maternity leave ended. Gibson took it personally; he considers Tina one of his closest friends despite seeing her so rarely outside the office. As soon as she said that, he began to think of quitting again. The idea of getting to know someone new in her position felt impossible. He'd rather start all over somewhere else.

"Good luck with Veda today," Tina says, as she shakes her closed Tupperware. "You'll do fine. All she's going to feel is regret for leaving such a great guy. You're gonna kill it." She says the last part the same way she does when he's about to head into a big pitch, and he watches her walk away both appreciating that her ass is getting bigger and wondering if they really do have a friendship that could survive outside work.

He stands in the hallway, scrolling all the dirty photos in his phone from Cammie. Several pages' worth. Does he have time to jerk off in the upstairs single-stall bathroom? Not enough time. In the elevator he imagines what he's going to do to Cammie after work, which doesn't calm the situation. But getting in the car and getting the *Just making sure we're still on for lunch* text from Veda shifts the vibe back to sombre reality.

He leaves with enough time to find parking on Dovercourt and hopefully not be late. He drives up and down from Dundas to Queen twice, something that would have enraged him in his previous life. The street is narrow to the point of almost being undrivable, with cyclists darting by him on both sides. Then a spot opens up right outside the restaurant. Veda used to hate how he was always late. He's surprised by how easy it is to have this planned encounter with her. It's been in his date book for a month—*Have lunch with Veda at the Cuban place.* Their place. When he wrote it down initially, his pen felt heavy. They were going on one month without speaking. That felt completely insane to him, to not speak to the person he'd spoken to for the majority of his adult life. It made him feel anxious, and then eventually, after a few days, he started to fantasize about how he would prepare to look so much happier when he showed up. To show her what she was missing. He thought about Veda every second of every day. She was a heavy blanket on his brain. But now that he has Cammie, Veda is gone. Erased almost. Except occasionally he misses her friendship, the way they'd sing the *Law & Order* theme song together, the molasses cookies she'd bake whenever she was on deadline, their shared jokes, the intimacies of everyday life— like knowing how to make her coffee, hearing about her dreams, the way that whenever he was sad she'd squeeze his arm and ask *What do you need right now?* Now he knows it's possible to have closeness with someone else, and to have even more of those intimacies, perhaps ones that matter more.

He opens up the Green P parking app, glancing at the clock—
four hours until he's supposed to pick up Cammie at Ossington
Station. Is Veda going to sense it in his face, that he's moved on?
He's nervous and excited to see her, but he feels less invested in the
outcome than ever. When they made this date he'd hoped they
might reconcile after some much-needed space. His biggest fear
was that she would replace him quickly with someone so much
better and that it might kill him. Even though of course he wants
her to be happy, but that kind of goodwill was hard to muster most
days. But today he hopes that she has met someone better, someone who drives her wild, so they will be on equal footing.

A few couples are seated on the patio, but he knows she'll be
inside because she hates the wind. He peeks over the health
inspection sign on the door and sees that she is already at their
usual table by the far wall, stirring a lemon with her straw in a tall
glass of water. There are only about six two-top tables in the whole
place. A Wilco album is playing that he hasn't heard in years.
They've changed the tablecloths from red-and-white gingham to
white and painted the walls a new colour, but he can't remember
what colour they used to be. An artist's charcoal rendering of vari-
ous seaside villages hangs on a wall where for years there had been
black-and-white photographs of horses. The old man who owns
the place sits behind the counter as other members of his family
work behind him in the kitchen. "Hey, Cameron," he says, and
Gibson doesn't correct him. It's been too many years. He's Cameron whenever he comes here. Gibson had been acutely aware of
Veda as soon as he'd opened the door but doesn't want to wave
awkwardly as he moves toward her; he performs a spectacle of
relaxed normalcy, though he feels like a towering monster trying
to move through the room and his shirt is already sticking to his

back. She has cut her hair to her shoulders and gotten reddish highlights. She looks both prettier and older.

"Wow, your hair," he says, still standing, hands on the back of his chair, wondering if they should hug. She doesn't make a move to stand up, so he sits down. The table wobbles.

"What, too much?" She scowls.

"No, no. It looks fantastic. You look great."

"I hadn't changed it in years. You know, I'm just trying new things these days."

"Same, same," he says, and pours himself a water, looking at the menu though he knows exactly what's on it. He always gets the pulled pork, she the grilled fish, and they share a side of plantains.

"I've started meditating, actually. And I'm taking a pottery class."

She says it in a way that sounds like she's trying to prove something to Gibson, like these new hobbies are accomplishments of some kind. She sounds so middle-aged, it pains him a little.

"That's cool. You getting the usual?"

"Yeah," she says, pulling some papers out of her purse. "So, maybe we should just get this stuff out of the way first, you know, the insurance papers, the mortgage. You just need to sign these, to make it official."

"Of course." He grabs them and pretends to read. The words swirl. She hands him a silver pen, the one with *Millcroft Inn* on the side, the hotel they always visited on their anniversaries. For some reason he drops it on the table and scrambles to get it before it rolls off, which makes him laugh in that way that you do when you're nervous and nothing is actually funny.

"You're much more relaxed than I thought you would be," Veda says in an accusatory tone.

"What do you mean?"

"I don't know. It was your idea to break up, but it's as if the day after you initiated it you regretted it. You actually having the balls to make the decision sort of set me free. It felt right, right away. But you know, the last time you were so mad."

Gibson cringes. The last time he saw her he was sobbing and begging her to come back to him.

"I just panicked. I'm fine now. Better, even. I just miss your friendship," he says. She raises her eyebrows. He realizes in that moment that she had expected him to show up distraught, to beg for reconciliation.

"What changed?"

"Time, I guess. And space."

"It hasn't been *that* long."

The server with the giant glasses lingers around them, seeming to understand she's about to interrupt something tense. "So, what will it be?" she asks brightly.

"I'll have the fish. No plantains," Veda says.

"We always share them. I can't eat all of them myself."

"Bring them home, then," Veda says, to her menu.

Gibson wonders then if she knows that he has someone to bring food home to. But he doesn't ask, just orders his usual. The rest of lunch goes fairly smoothly, all things considered. He's curious if she's met someone but also doesn't want to know.

"How has it been, living alone? You've never lived alone," he says.

"It's lonely sometimes. I think I hear you playing video games in the other room. It's so odd." She starts to cry. It's an abrupt shift. He reaches out to touch her hand but she pulls it away. She twists her hair the way she does when she's nervous.

"Dammit. Dammit. I told myself I wouldn't cry."

"It's okay. I've been sad too."

"You don't seem sad at all," she says.

"I am, I am sad," he says, but he isn't convincing.

Gibson stuffs a whole plantain slice in his mouth and then tries to pretend he did that on purpose, chewing slowly, as though this weren't the person who has seen him at his most vulnerable—after his hernia surgery, when he had food poisoning, when he broke his arm.

"I've been going to the gym sometimes," he offers. He can feel his phone vibrate in his pocket. Over and over. He's dying to see if it's from Cammie but refrains. He's started getting turned on just by the sound of his phone going off lately, because ninety-five percent of the time it is from her.

"You can get that," Veda says, making an exaggerated effort to look away from the table.

"Nah, it's probably work. Tina falls apart whenever I go for a long lunch."

They eat in silence for a minute or two. He finishes all the plantains and feels uncomfortable. The place empties out a bit. He wishes he'd ordered a beer. He's been drinking more since the divorce.

"So," Veda says, as though preparing herself to bring up something heavy. Gibson's heart starts pounding—here it comes. She has a new boyfriend. He takes a deep breath. He tries to make an open and accepting facial expression, while making a smile shape in hot sauce on top of his remaining rice.

"Julian and Kelly are having their annual Labour Day barbecue Sunday. I guess I wondered if you were going."

He exhales while taking a forkful of half the smile.

"Oh, definitely, I never miss it. Unless you don't want me to," he says. Kelly is her friend. But Julian is his *best* friend. Kelly and Veda are only friends because of his and Julian's long-standing friendship.

"Okay, no, maybe I'll come for a bit. That wouldn't be weird, would it?"

"Of course not," he says, even though he assumed she wouldn't come.

Gibson pays the cheque while Veda is in the bathroom, which he thinks is a generous thing to do, but Veda seems annoyed by it when she comes back.

"I know this is ludicrous but I feel as though you're trying to win the breakup," she says, pulling on her cardigan.

"Uh, that's not how I feel at all. I'm just trying to be kind. I want us to be friends."

"Maybe we can be, eventually. It's too raw right now."

"Okay," he says, and turns to leave the restaurant.

"See? Even that. If I'd suggested we not be friends last month I feel like you'd have yelled and cried."

"Are you upset that I am being civil and calm? Do you want me to feel bad?"

"No, of course not. I want you to be happy, I want things to be okay for you. I guess I'm just surprised by how this went. I came prepared to state my boundaries, to check in, and I guess I didn't expect it to go like this."

Gibson couldn't stop himself from snorting.

"You're upset that I'm not a mess. That I'm seeing how good a decision this was."

She looks wounded at that, but nods. "I'm sorry, I'm just being honest."

She starts to cry. Gibson isn't sure what to say. "It's been the opposite with me; it's gotten harder, not easier."

"Are you saying you regret the split?"

She holds his gaze for a few moments, then shakes her head.

Even though he agrees with her, that they can't go back, it still hurts a little to see her resolve.

"Okay, then."

"It's strange that the actual divorce won't be final for a year."

"A year feels like a long time, doesn't it?"

"Sometimes, yeah."

They share an awkward hug goodbye, one she doesn't seem eager to break. It is such a role reversal—she was so stoic the day he packed the moving van. She told him to stop crying and carrying on and to be mature about the decision he'd ultimately made. Gibson feels protective of Veda as it starts to rain a little bit.

"Are you going to be okay?" he asks, as she finally pulls away. "Do you want a ride, or did you bike here?"

"You were so good at that, always making sure I had what I needed. I have my bike, it's cool." She rubs her eyes. He opens his driver door, watches her unlock her bike. Then she turns toward him again. "Gibson, I feel like you're not even present. Like this either isn't affecting you emotionally or you're totally dissociated."

"No, of course not. This is a huge deal, Veda."

She doesn't seem satisfied with this answer, but there's nothing much else he can do. He's feeling antsy, desperate to check his phone, so he just says, "Bye, then."

The first text was a fully nude photo of Cammie. *Hope you miss me today.* She was on her bed, wearing heels and that's all. It came in right at noon, when she knew Gibson was meeting Veda, so the timing was a bit weird. Maybe insensitive? But he chalks it up to her being young, and maybe jealous. Could she actually be jealous? Gibson had previously never sent a dick pic in his life and now he feels almost expert level at it. He is so preoccupied by the photo he hardly feels anything as Veda bikes away in his periphery.

The texts that arrived after the photo were *Why no reply?* and then *Fuck, James is home early and he's in a MOOD. I'm hiding in the closet and I'm going to slip out the back door. Can you come get me?*

Absolutely, he texts back. On the way he fantasizes about finding this James and punching him in the nuts and making him leave her apartment for good. He would carry her over his shoulder. *Oh my god, who am I becoming?*

He pulls up in front of the address she gave him on a tree-lined street near St. Clair and Oakwood. He's squinting at the house number just as a tall, football-player-looking brute exits the side door carrying a duffel bag. He throws it in an old-model red Toyota Tercel that has one window duct-taped with a garbage bag and slams the door; when he turns the engine over the music blares and he pulls out of the driveway. For a second he's side by side with Gibson's pickup and he glances at him for a beat. Gibson's heart pounds. He cannot fight this dude. He can't fight any dude. They lock eyes. The guy—James?—turns the volume down. "Good luck, bud. She will ruin your fucking life."

Gibson shakes his head like he doesn't know what James is talking about, unsure how to respond. Thankfully he doesn't have to. James peels away. Gibson opens the car door and stands on the street for a beat, orienting himself. There's an older lady sitting on the porch across the street, staring at him eerily. He has a brief moment where he has an instinct to flee. He'll remember this moment later, recount it breathlessly to anyone who will listen—*I knew, something in me knew.* But then a text comes in. *Almost here?*

Yup, out front.

She bounds out, holding a big purse to her chest, mascara smeared down her face. She jumps up into the passenger side.

Gibson feels dumb asking, as he knows the answer. "Are you okay?"

She shrugs, sniffing a bit. Her knees are skinned. "Did he get violent with you?"

"No, not this time." Gibson can hardly hear above the roar in his ears.

"He stole money from me, and he turned the landlord against me, which really sucks because I got fired last night."

"What? Why? You've worked at that bar forever." That is a lot to take in.

"It's a long story," she says, doing up her seatbelt, "but basically the new night manager hates me for some reason and kept fucking with my shifts and I got mad at her, which you can't do to Kim, she'll make your life hell. And she steals from the final count, I know she does. I've seen her do it. But she told everyone it was me."

"Uh, you can't let her do that! Let's go, right now. Talk to Tom, you've known Tom forever."

"I just want to be rid of that place anyway. Turn over a new leaf. It's a sign from the universe."

"What can I do to make things better?" This is a question he learned to ask from Veda. She puts her hand on his knee. He feels like his chest is full of bees. Nothing this dramatic has ever really happened to him. He feels caught up in it. He wants to fight her ex-boyfriend, her boss, anyone.

Cammie smiles at him. "You're so good," she says, leaning over and kissing him.

"Where should we go?"

"Let's get ice cream!" She shouts it, like a little girl. It's a strange contrast to Veda, how stoic and set in her ways she is now, how the wrinkle between her eyes has become so much more pronounced since the divorce.

Gibson drives to Bakerbots, a place she's never been before that usually has long lines. It's early enough that they don't have to wait. She is so impressed by it—he insists they have the banana pudding ice cream between two chocolate cookies, the best flavour. Then he realizes it's impossible to eat and stay desirable, so he lets her eat it all, pretends to be full from lunch. She recounts the story of James, how he was going to be a pro boxer but got one too many head injuries. That she's been paying all their bills this year and is maxed out. She was afraid to let him go at first, but when she met Gibson, it all felt so dumb, him and her.

"I thought that too! That's how I felt about Veda! It's like you removed her from my heart."

Cammie grins. "I forgot to ask you how lunch went. That was today, right?"

"It was fine. I think we might be friends, someday."

She puts her hand on Gibson's shoulder, plays with his hair a bit. Between licks of melting ice cream she drops, "I'm in love with you." She says it like *The sky is blue* and then she kisses him. He feels it with his whole chest. When she pulls away she's shy, a face in full blush.

"I know it's pretty soon to say that, but I know when something is right. This is bigger than us."

Maybe that's what this explosive feeling is. Not just lust. Maybe it's the love Gibson has been wanting but was too afraid to look for. The kind of love people write songs about. He didn't have movie love with Veda, especially not after the first few months. When it's real, you know it. Later, a therapist will call this *a red flag*.

———————

Cammie spends the weekend at his place. He's getting used to the way she cuddles up to him in sleep and doesn't let go, like a grippy little barnacle that smells like bergamot body spray and beer. On

Sunday morning, as he's frying a pan of bacon and she's showing him how to use a squeeze bottle to make perfect pancakes, he tells her that if she doesn't want to go back to her old place, given all the conflict with her ex, she can stay with him as long as she wants. He doesn't expect her to say yes, but she does. She makes a smiley face pancake.

"You're such a good person," she says, "so generous and thoughtful. Of course I'd love to stay."

He gets a brief flicker of panic when he turns away to tear off a piece of paper towel for the bacon. He imagines telling Julian that she's moving in. It's obviously too soon. He takes strips of bacon out of the pan and lays them on the paper towel.

"It will be easier for you to save up and look for a new place if you're here, you know, safe and comfortable." He presses the paper towel down onto the bacon to absorb the grease. She flips the smiley face pancake and looks down.

"Yeah, you're totally right." He can't tell if she thought he was asking her to move in more permanently and is disappointed or if she wouldn't have thought that in the first place.

They bring their plates out to the back patio but instead of sitting down, Cammie goes back inside to get a scoop of raw peanuts to line up on the wooden ledge for the squirrels. Watching her delight in this ritual makes Gibson think about children, how Cammie's easygoing, cheerful nature might translate into motherhood.

"So, do you know if you want kids someday?" he asks as she sits down at the table and pours them both mimosas. She gives him a sly look, holding eye contact as she drinks.

"Why, that's not what I mean when I call you Daddy, but yes, of course I want kids."

"Not everyone does."

"I know, I know. But I always assumed I'd be a mother someday. And honestly"—she puts her hand on his leg—"it sounds crazy, but the second time we hung out I kept thinking about what a great dad you'd be, you know? We'd make a good team. You're so kind. And I'm such a scrapper. We'd give a kid a good life."

"We would, wouldn't we?" he hears himself saying, though he knows it's premature. It's okay to daydream, right?

"Your ex didn't want kids?"

He contemplates telling her about the miscarriage, about how much they wanted to have a kid. But he holds the details close and just shakes his head.

"I had a kid once," she says, "but I was young. I gave it up for adoption."

"Oh my god," he says.

"It's okay. It was the right thing to do. I think about her all the time, though."

"Do you know anything about where she went?"

"No, they wouldn't tell me. They ripped her away from me. My mother made sure I didn't know anything. She was very controlling. She still won't tell me."

"But you're older now, surely you have rights. And the dad."

"It was complicated," she says, and starts to eat her breakfast like they're not talking about anything traumatic.

"I'm so sorry," he says, utterly heartbroken for the teenaged Cammie he can imagine in his head.

"And now, you know, the doctors aren't sure I can even have kids, after all the chemo," she says.

He feels crushed by this news but tries not to show it.

"I'm actually having some tests done next week, so I'll know for sure."

"Good, that's great for you, to know," he says.

She gets up and sits on his lap.

"But why don't we roll the dice now?" she says, and puts her hand on his crotch. He laughs, trying to gauge how serious she is. When they get to the bedroom, though, and make a game of it, he doesn't use a condom but he pulls out at the last moment.

She looks disappointed. "I told you it was okay to come in me."

"I wasn't sure," he says, "if you were just dirty talking, you know, if it was just a fantasy. I didn't want to do anything you didn't really consent to."

"You're such a good guy," she says, but in a way he isn't sure is sincere.

His phone timer goes off, to remind him about the barbecue at Julian's. He doesn't even think about whether or not to bring her; leaving her seems absurd. She's totally into it until he reminds her that Veda might come.

———————

It's fall, but still summertime hot outside. Gibson drinks a bottle of blue Gatorade while they walk north toward Julian's neighbour-hood. Cammie drinks a tall can. Julian and Kelly live in one of those houses on the north side of Davenport, built at the top of the hill, making it necessary to climb three steep staircases to reach the front door. Cammie gets quieter the closer they get, until she pauses at the bottom of Julian's steps.

"What if they don't like me?" she asks.

"Nah, don't worry, everyone's chill. Who could ever not like you?" But he is also worried. She is young, and he can only imag-ine what Veda might think. He's also acutely aware, all of a sudden, that his friends have all been to grad school and that maybe they'll be snobs. More possible is that Cammie will find them dull.

At first it's fine. Cammie is really impressed by his friends. When they walk around the side of the house and into the yard, he is taken aback at how his female friends act upon seeing Cammie for the first time. Julian and his guy friends who'd met her at the breakfast patio mostly smirk and act friendly. Kelly and the others do not hide their shock very well. "Wow, you are a gorgeous one," Kelly says, looking Cammie up and down. Cammie giggles and strikes a model pose. Gibson gives Kelly a look that says *Stop it.*

Gibson loves his friends, he'd take a bullet for most of them, but Cammie is a cool, hipster type of girl with her white cowboy boots and her stick-and-poke tattoos. Will she text her friends about her boring boyfriend's boring friends? He is suddenly aware that other than her co-workers he doesn't know any of her friends. She doesn't speak about any. Maybe she's one of those girls who only has boyfriends.

But she seems immediately taken in by the grandeur of the house, appreciating the painting above Julian and Kelly's mantelpiece, which Gibson has never noticed before, impressed by the sound system and TV, genuinely interested in getting to know everyone. Gibson is most comfortable around people he already knows; he'd never be able to just walk right into a stranger's house, let alone a new date's best friends', and look so comfortable. Especially not when he was her age. He's only seen the outside of her basement apartment, but from what he can tell, she doesn't seem to have a lot of money. But he watches Kelly react to her fancy handbag, and her boots are apparently some kind of impressive brand he's never heard of. As he watches them chat about her outfit, he sees Cammie a bit differently. Maybe she's not just a kid.

Julian and Kelly were the first in their friend group to buy a house; they used to joke that they became adults first, but really they just have more money. It used to bother Gibson a lot, but he's mellowed about it. He's not too bad off, but normal middle class in Owen Sound was basically broke in Toronto. Before the divorce he and Veda had bought a small condo and were saving for a house but knew they'd have to go to the suburbs to afford anything. Kelly is an academic, a newly tenured professor, and Julian works in radio production.

Gibson and Cammie arrive right after Julian's sister Justine and her wife, Tess, whom they join in the backyard next to the fire pit and the outdoor bar. Julian and Kelly have the kind of outdoor furniture that looks indistinguishable from indoor furniture. Cammie becomes fast friends with their dog, a goldendoodle named Egg who generally never likes anyone but crawls up on her lap.

The vibe in the backyard is relaxed, and Cammie charms every new person she meets—giving out nicknames and cracking jokes and beating Julian at ping-pong. When she goes to the bathroom, Kelly sits down in Cammie's chair and leans in close. "Okay, I get why you like her. She's fun! Like really fun."

"Right? I'm having a good time right now."

"You needed it. A summer fling. Someone younger. I get it."

"No, no. This is real," he says, taking a too-large spoonful of potato salad and nearly choking.

"You have barely been divorced for like two hours. Take your time."

Julian, hovering nearby, leans in. "It's just, we worry about you, is all."

"Nah, nothing to worry about anymore." He takes another bite he doesn't want.

Cammie is suddenly there again, and they all go silent as she sits on Gibson's lap. She chugs the rest of her beer and then stands up to crush it with her boot, which would have looked like a dumb redneck thing if he did it but seems sexy and funny when she does it. Gibson's dad would probably call her "a wild one."

"It's okay, you can talk about how much you like me while I'm here," she laughs.

"I do like seeing my boy happy," Julian says.

"Oh, I definitely make him happy," she says, leaning in to give him a make-out kiss. Cammie pulls away and says, "I know, let's play two truths and a lie."

Everyone is drunk enough to be amused, but Gibson feels a little embarrassed that she suggested a juvenile game, which she can sense.

"It's a getting-to-know-you activity. I did it when I facilitated groups back in college," she says.

Before they can respond, she gets up and gathers the whole party around their chairs by the fire pit and explains the rules of the game—you tell three things about yourself, one has to be a lie, and everyone guesses which one. As she talks, Gibson takes in the fact that Cammie isn't just a great flirt, she can command a room. She has been slowly charming everyone at the party, really zeroing in on them and making them feel special. She already has an inside joke with Kelly. Justine, always the drunkest at any party, appears to be matching Cammie drink for drink, and is especially enamoured. Tess declines to play; instead she lingers on the edge of the group to take photographs. At some point at every gathering, Justine and Tess have some sort of blow-out fight. But they never break up.

Cammie says, "I'll start! I met Brad Pitt in a coffee shop. I sang backup on an Arcade Fire song. And I have a twin sister who doesn't speak to me."

She turns to Gibson. "You can't play, you already know the lie!"

He knows she doesn't have a twin sister, so he keeps his mouth shut as he watches his friends try to guess—everyone says Brad Pitt, except for Justine, who guesses the backup singer.

"Nope, that one's true! I don't have a twin sister."

She launches into the story about Brad Pitt in the coffee shop. Everyone is rapt.

"Which Arcade Fire song?" Tess asks, soberly, joining the group.

" 'Reflektor.' "

"You must be older than you look."

"Guilty! And you know, I never use any moisturizer. I think that's actually the secret."

"So you were in Louisiana?" Tess asks, and Cammie looks at her oddly.

"Tess, Jesus. It's my turn!" Justine says, cuddling up to Cammie. "Okay, I once smoked a joint with Beck. I had scarlet fever twice. I can speak four languages."

As the game continues, Gibson notices Tess whispering something to Julian before they walk off together. As Gibson desperately tries to think of a truth that would be interesting enough for Cammie and not immediately identifiable by his closest friends, he decides to fake a trip to the bathroom. He doesn't want to break the seal yet. When he walks into the kitchen, Julian and Tess go quiet. "What's going on? I know that look," Gibson says, popping open a bag of chips and refilling a bowl.

"Nothing."

"We need to tell him."

"None of our business, Tess."

"Gibson, Cammie did not sing on that album. I know the guy who produced that record. She's not in the credits either. And she would have been, what, nineteen? Come on. I get a vibe, Gibson. A liar vibe."

"You're paranoid! And just because she isn't credited doesn't mean it's impossible."

"I would bet my entire life savings that she is not on that record. They recorded it in Louisiana. She didn't seem to know that. Something is not right with her."

Gibson takes in this information, feeling unsteady. It does seem a bit odd that she didn't mention it before.

————

When they go back outside, Tess peppers Cammie with questions about her music career. "What are you, a cop?" Justine interrupts to chide her. Everyone gets uncomfortable.

Cammie has an answer for everything. It makes Gibson relieved, how well she can handle herself. He thinks about backing her up more emphatically, but she seems fine. Eventually she shrugs and says, "Look, I don't know what to tell you. I was there. I sang on the song."

"Okay," Tess says, but everyone can tell she still doesn't believe her.

"I apologize for my wife. She's a true-crime junkie and is looking for stories everywhere!" Justine says. Tess gives her a look that says this year's fight is *on*, and they retreat inside just as the gate swings open and all heads turn toward the entrance to the yard.

It's Veda.

"Hey, guys," she says. She looks incredible, like she got a blowout and a new dress. Kelly gets up to hug her. Gibson also stands, awkwardly, unsure what to do. Veda knows everyone there except Cammie. When she realizes Gibson isn't going to introduce her, she goes right ahead. "I'm Cammie," she says. They shake hands. And then everyone watches Veda slowly realize who she might be. Her face goes red but she remains expressionless.

"I'll bring the salad inside," she says, as Kelly quickly follows behind her.

Gibson is about to make an excuse for them to leave when Cammie turns to Gibson and pulls him aside.

"I've got a pain in my side," she says, motioning to her abdomen.

"What kind of pain? Is it dull or constant?" he asks.

"A bit of both? Sharp, really. I need to be careful, you know, because of how I just finished treatment."

"Of course, oh my gosh, want me to take you home? I've got a hot water bottle." She winces and grabs at her side. "Or should I take you to the ER? I know you should be extra careful right now."

"You have a lot going on here," she says. "I don't want to be intrusive. I don't think Veda wants me here."

"We're all adults, it will be fine," he lies, but she continues around the side of the house. "Plus, I'm totally ready to leave. I'd rather be with you."

He trails after her down the steep steps onto the street.

"Let me drive you!"

"We walked here." She is slurring her words a little and her mood seems to have turned now that they're alone. She's had a lot to drink and he doesn't want to leave her for that reason as well.

"I can use Julian's car. He won't mind, just let me go ask him."

"I said no," she says.

"It's your right side, it could be appendicitis."

"No, no. I've felt this before. Don't worry. This stuff is old hat for me." She winces a little as she speaks.

He tries to pull her close, but she won't have it.

"I told you, I like to be alone when I don't feel well. Can you just go back inside? My place is close, James isn't there. I can rest and call my doctor."

"I can't let you leave alone in this state."

"Jesus, give the hero act a rest!"

Gibson backs up, hands in the air. "Okay, sorry," he mumbles. He climbs the stairs up to the landing again and watches her cross the street and wander down Shaw. She's weaving a little.

He spends the next hour inside playing a video game with Julian while Veda is outside with the rest of the guests. Eventually he wanders back outside and sees her talking with Tess.

"So I hear your girl is some kinda drama queen," Veda says. Her eyes are saucered. She never usually drinks, and when she does she can get a little mean.

"No, it was a misunderstanding."

Tess snorts. Veda and Tess share a look that makes Gibson feel about five years old.

"Guys, be nice, okay? This hasn't exactly been an easy year for any of us."

"The theme of this year's barbecue is 'uncomfortable feelings.'" Tess laughs.

Gibson goes back inside and smokes a joint with Julian. He doesn't want to leave the party, be the one who is exiled from his friend group. He washes dishes with Kelly, who says, "Well, everyone lies sometimes. Even if it isn't true, it's innocuous. She was outnumbered, the new girl; everyone is bound to be a little insecure."

Gibson tells her that she's been through so much in her life; he tells her about Cammie's recent remission from cancer.

"That is really weird," Kelly says, drying the last dish and placing it in the cupboard.

"Why?"

"Because Tess said that Cammie reminded her of a woman from her office who lied about having cancer. She said they were so similar and ever since she got so burned by that woman, she says she has a sixth sense about these things. And then Justine said she's just paranoid and has PTSD from it, because I guess she gave the woman a lot of money and emotional support, and so now she imagines everyone is terrible but statistically, it would be pretty rare to know two cancer liars in one life."

"I don't think she's lying. Only a monster would lie about that, and she is not a monster. She's made me feel alive for the first time in years. And she's so sweet. She remembers everything. I feel really cared for."

Gibson never speaks to his friends this way. Even through the haze of all-day drinking, he feels embarrassed.

"It's okay, man. Your feelings are valid," says Julian, trying to be supportive.

Gibson decides to sleep on the couch in their basement, which is where he originally stayed after the breakup. He falls into a drunken sleep, waking up before dawn to several texts from Cammie. *I'm in a lot of pain. I'm going to the ER at Western.*

Gibson sits up and calls her back. No answer. He sends multiple texts. No answer. He paces around, unsure what to do, picturing the worst reasons why she wouldn't be answering her phone. Finally he calls the ER at the hospital and asks for her by name. "She went in around three A.M., and she hasn't contacted me since. I'm worried she's not okay," he says in a panic. The nurse comes back on the line and in a practised, calm voice says, "No one by that name has been to the ER in the last twenty-four hours."

He calls St. Joe's, then a few more hospitals. Same thing. Eventually he goes back to his place and gets in the truck and drives to the ER bay at the Western. He goes inside and searches the waiting room and then asks the nurse in person. No one by that name. He sits in his truck and keeps texting and calling—nothing. He goes to her apartment and bangs on the door. No answer. Where is she?

6

Shelby gets out of the Uber on a dark street, a bit worried that if he drives away she'll be stranded. She turns her phone back on. Then she hears her name being called, as if from the heavens. She turns around and around trying to find the voice, like a dumb extra in a horror movie, before she gets a text. *I'm up on top of the school building. There's a ladder beside the blue dumpster.*

Shelby looks around, unable to find the dumpster. She walks toward the wall of the school; still no ladder. Eventually Cammie has to climb back down. Though Cammie sounds a bit drunk, she walks confidently.

"I'm afraid of heights," Shelby says. It's easier than saying she is generally afraid of everything.

"I swear, you won't regret it."

Shelby watches Cammie climb back up the rickety metal ladder, made of chipped black and rusty paint. She pauses halfway up to look down.

"I can't!" Shelby calls up. "I really don't want to climb a building in the middle of the night. I don't even really, uh, know you."

Cammie laughs in a way that hurts Shelby's feelings. She's very sensitive to being thought of as ridiculous or overly cautious, and it takes a lot for her to openly disagree with someone like this. It has taken years of therapy for Shelby to stop doing things because she's afraid to not be seen as nice or accommodating. There's a moment, looking up at Cammie, when Shelby is reminded of a girl she was briefly friends with at theatre camp when she was twelve. Samantha was a tough tomboy with a side shave and combat boots who Shelby was immediately drawn to—later she figured out why—but she was also a bit afraid of her at first and Samantha could tell and even seemed to like it. "You're so sweet, you're such a sweet kid," Samantha would say, as though she weren't also twelve and a half. The camp ran every day from nine to three in an apartment above a store on Yonge Street. There was a big open room for the workshops, and a small office full of junk where Cheryl, the director of the camp, smoked and drank diet sodas and the walls were covered in eight-by-ten headshots of child actors, several of whom had been on *Degrassi*, which was Shelby's first career goal. Samantha had been to the camp the year before and was buddies with Cheryl, who often gave her food and let her play games on the computer when she went out for lunch.

The day was divided into several workshops: movement, improv, scenework, and dance. Scenework was Shelby's favourite class but they often had to pair up, which made her nervous. Shelby was uncool and Samantha was tough, and they often ended up together. Only later on did she realize it was her first S/M encounter. Samantha pushed Shelby's boundaries that summer. The bitchy, wealthy theatre girls didn't like Samantha, and she knew it. But there was middle-class Shelby, in the middle of them, who also didn't fit in with the girls who were going to Club Med and wore two-hundred-dollar jeans. Slowly Samantha had realized Shelby didn't know how to say no to her, and whether she was opportunistic or just lonely, she used it to her advantage. Shelby invited her over for dinner the first week of camp when they were just getting to know each other, and Samantha fell in love with Shelby's mom. Once Samantha told her mom that she was in foster care, she told her she was welcome anytime. And so she came over every day, even when Shelby strongly hinted she'd rather go home alone. Shelby found herself in several uncomfortable positions that summer—shoplifting at lunch when she didn't want to; doing partner scenes where Samantha made her play the male role, which made her furious in a way she couldn't describe; and watching Sam hanging out with her mother, who seemed to let Samantha get away with anything because of "her sad home life." Later Shelby would understand that her mother was being kind, but at the time she felt jealous at having to share her with a girl who called her a spoiled baby when her mom wasn't in the room. In the end she realized that Samantha was lonely and pushed people around because she had to fight for everything in her foster home. Eventually, when camp ended, Shelby just stopped answering her phone calls. That passivity was her only way to make her feelings known.

So now adult Shelby feels stubborn, on the ground outside a weird building. Why should she crawl up the side of a building?

"I prefer the ground!"

Cammie doesn't taunt her, she just ascends the ladder and says, "Okay, I'm not trying to push you to do something you're not comfortable with. But just answer me this: What do you have to lose? The view up there is incredible. I thought you hadn't left your apartment in months. What would make a more exciting chapter in your memoir?"

Shelby thinks about what she has to lose, really. Days spent googling symptoms, missing Kate, watching seven episodes of

Law & Order: SVU? This would at least be a novel way to die. She takes a deep breath and follows her.

Fuck it.

When she gets to the first roof, Cammie is already across it, climbing up another ladder to get even higher. The surface on the way to the second ladder is made of gravel. Shelby feels like she's on the moon, even though the moon itself is high in the sky, full and glaring at her as she acts like a trespassing teenager.

Shelby eventually makes it to the top of the second ladder. *I did it!* Cammie is sitting on a blanket near the far edge. Shelby tentatively joins her, kneeling on the edge of the raggedy quilt, still a bit breathless. Then the exhilaration passes and her real personality sets in again. She doesn't even know this woman. Cammie could stab her and leave her for dead. Birds would peck at her. No one would find her for years.

"Morgan used to bring me here after we'd close the bar," Cammie says, handing her a half-full bottle of wine. "She'd say it helped keep things in perspective, you know, how small we really are."

Shelby looks at the bottle—it's a fancy French wine she's never heard of. Should she share this woman's germs? Can she rub the top of the bottle with her shirt sleeve real quick, without being noticed? Cammie stares right at her, as if testing her somehow. "I'm not really supposed to drink on my Celexa," Shelby says.

"Everyone's on that shit and everyone drinks. Don't worry about it."

Shelby is never really convinced by these types of arguments but she feels shy, so she takes a sip, trying not to let the bottle's lip touch hers. Then a slightly bigger sip. *Doesn't the alcohol neutralize the germs anyway?*

"So, how was your night?" Shelby asks, as though making

casual small talk at a cocktail party and not trespassing with a rela-
tive stranger.

"Well, to be honest, not too fabulous. I got fired yesterday. The
new manager is a real piece of work. Last week I overheard her
calling Tom a fag and I called her on it."

"That's fucked up! She should be the one who gets fired," Shelby
says, passing the bottle back to her.

Cammie gulps the wine like it's water. "She tried to claim she
can say it because she's been around the queer community for
decades. But she was using it as an insult, and she didn't want me
to overhear. Then she made my life hell all week, accused me of
stealing. So now I'm out. After almost nine years of working there."
She puts the bottle down and leans back, making movements like
a snow angel.

"That doesn't seem fair. She should be disciplined for her
homophobia," Shelby offers, though she knows it's a naive thing to
say. She leans back as well, staring up at the moon.

"Look, if I could be gay, I would be. Sure seems a lot easier."

Shelby nods, although it's a sentiment she's heard a lot and it
usually annoys her. "Double PMS is a tragedy, quite frankly," she
offers. She feels rocks or debris poking up at her back. She could
be getting sliced up right now. She sits up, tries to brush her back.

"My sister was gay. She used to tell me she thought that I was
in love with Morgan."

"Were you?"

"Maybe sometimes."

"How old was your sister? The dyke community is so small,
maybe I knew her?"

"She didn't live here. She was mostly in Vancouver the last few
years."

Cammie sits up, offers the bottle back to Shelby. They sit across from each other, legs crossed. It reminds Shelby of drama camp again, that game where you have to mirror each other.

"Do you have a boyfriend now?"

"Yeah. He's older. It's kind of new. I'm crashing with him a lot right now, actually. Not ideal but I don't have a lot of other options. We had a big fight tonight, actually. He took me to meet his friends and he didn't stick up for me when they made fun of my age. They're all older, academics. I want someone who is loyal, you know?" She points to some bruising on her leg. "I don't always know how to pick them."

"Jesus, that from the new guy?"

"No, from my ex, James. He was a fighter. He had a head injury, so he'd get violent sometimes, like a child."

"That's awful. Must have been really traumatic for you."

"Well, we all have our flaws. I'm no picnic."

Shelby appreciates that, although a lot of awful things have happened to Cammie, she often makes comments like this. "I like that you can see both sides of things," she says.

"I noticed that about you, too. You're very diplomatic," Cammie says.

"I like how you acknowledge that not everything is black and white," Shelby says, in a way that reminds her of an HR exercise they did at work where they had to compliment each other's strong suits and mirror each other. She takes another sip of wine.

"The new guy, he's nicer? What's his name?"

"Gibson. Yeah, he's okay."

"Not in love?"

"Maybe? Too soon to tell."

"I can ask around, see if anyone's looking for a roommate or anything?"

"Nah, it's okay. I always land on my feet."

Shelby notices that when Camilla lifts up her sleeves there are white lines on her wrists. She stares at them too long to not be noticed. Cammie runs a finger over the cut marks but doesn't say anything. Shelby takes another big swig from the bottle, no longer caring about their shared germs. There's a thrill to the feeling of not caring about it, and an intimacy, too. Her spirit truly soars whenever it has a moment of letting go, of saying *Fuck it!* to the obsessions that have always burdened her. In this moment she feels like stopping her medications, so she can drink wine and not worry about the interactions, so she can see what her brain is like naturally. It has been so long since she was first prescribed them at age twenty-four, in her last year of university. They allowed her two good years of reprieve from anxiety, but it came lurking back. She's been forgetting to take them regularly since Kate died anyway.

"It's funny, we're kind of both in a place where we could make big changes in our lives, you know? You with a new job, me with . . . god, just anything new. Should we change our lives and live as outlaws?"

"Been there, done that," says Cammie, in a way that makes Shelby curious, but she doesn't want to pry. There is something a bit dangerous-feeling about Cammie. An unpredictability. It's intoxicating to be around after months of solitude and sameness.

"I just need to find something to pay the bills, get my own place. I do not want to rely on a man."

"Oh no, definitely do not. I'll help you find something. What are you interested in, besides service gigs?"

"I don't know, I've always wanted to work in entertainment, I guess, like TV or film."

"I have a friend who produces reality shows. Want me to ask her if she's hiring?"

"Sure! That would be amazing."

They finish the wine and Cammie suggests Shelby throw the bottle against the concrete wall.

"Why?"

"It is very satisfying, trust me! Any anger you feel will dissolve with it."

She throws it halfheartedly at first, and Cammie runs to pick up the still-intact bottle and hand it back to her. "Really throw it. Like you want to kill it!"

Shelby lets the bottle have it and indeed the sound of it splintering into a million pieces feels so great that she jumps up in the air and claps like an idiot.

Cammie howls and hoots into the night. They must look like wolves running wild on top of the city. Eventually they climb down the rickety ladder, and when they reach the dumpster on the ground, Cammie reaches into it and pulls out a strange shape that slowly reveals itself as an oversized ceramic statue of a dog. A collie.

"Would you like a dog? She is magnificent!"

"I would love a dog! Coach Taylor can have a friend," Shelby says, cradling it as though it were truly mammalian.

"Let's call her Nina," Cammie says.

They call a cab, and while they ride south through the now-bare streets, Shelby sends an email to Olive asking if they need any production assistants. She insists Cammie not go back to the (maybe?) bad boyfriend's house. Instead they sit on her porch and drink more wine and put Nina on the top step of the porch as the new guard dog. She sets Cammie up on the pull-out couch in the basement, taking vintage quilts out of the old dresser in the corner to tuck her in like she's a child.

By morning Shelby is scrolling View It and printing out listings for apartments and inspirational blog posts about starting over and going through your Saturn return. She feels imbued with purpose, trying to help Cammie out. By the time Cammie wakes up she has made them plates of scrambled eggs and fruit salad, Coach Taylor sitting below Cammie hoping for the gift of dropped food. Cammie's phone buzzes nonstop.

"Everything okay? I don't mind if you answer."

"Just my boyfriend, trying to apologize. Not giving him the satisfaction. This is so nice, you're such a good person," Cammie says, before proceeding to eat breakfast like she hasn't eaten in weeks. Every few bites she gives a piece of egg or toast to Coach Taylor, cementing her place as beloved guest forever.

"You can stay anytime, my place is your place. Maybe Gibson can come over for dinner sometime? So we can all meet?" Shelby says, retrieving the key she used to leave for the dog walker from the junk drawer and handing it to Cammie. Shelby has always been anxious, too cautious, but sometimes she has these impulsive moments when she takes chances on people. When she first met Kate she bought her a new laptop when hers got stolen, and they'd only known each other a week. But she needed one and Shelby had the money—why be greedy? She feels that way now. Here is this girl who is grieving, who is generous with her time and advice, and she needs the help that Shelby can actually provide. It fills her with purpose.

Cammie tears up when she looks at the key.

"Yeah, maybe. Thanks for the key. It means so much that you trust me," she says. "I've really pushed my family away since the diagnosis."

"What diagnosis?"

Cammie spears a slice of avocado and stares at it as she speaks.

"I am officially in remission, as of a few weeks ago, from kidney cancer. But don't tell the group. I don't want a pity party."

Shelby feels a tiny twinge in her gut. It's a twinge that says *You don't really know this person.* Cammie tells the group so many deeply personal things. Why not this one? She pushes it away as Cammie tells her story. Shelby is being paranoid; she's forgotten how to relate to another human being. As soon as she has the feeling, she forgets it, not thinking about it again until a few weeks later.

"I feel like we met each other at the exact right time," Cammie says, pulling Shelby in for a hug. "You've just lost someone, so have I. Sometimes the universe just lines up the people we need, and all we have to do is pay attention."

"I think you're right," Shelby says.

Shelby feels a swell of appreciation for Cammie as she watches her walk down the front steps, stopping to pet Nina, and cross the overgrown front yard. She chats with the squirrel that has taken up residence in the neglected bird feeder on the front gate that Kate used to care for.

Shelby wants to be as free as Cammie looks. She wants to feel all the feelings, even bad ones. Lately she has only felt anxiety and numbness, vaulting between the two unpredictably.

———

She sits at her desk and opens her laptop. She has an email from her boss asking when she'll be returning. She sends her a quick note to say she'll be back next week. One from her mother she doesn't want to open. Her mother only emails if she has issues to discuss that she lacks the courage to say in person. She reads the first few sentences only: *I'm writing because I am concerned about your well-being. You should be back to regular life by now. Even if you don't feel it, you should fake it until you make it. You didn't die. Life goes on!* She stops reading when she feels like the email is just going to be things you'd read embroidered on pillows in a gift shop geared to WASPy ladies like her mother. She clicks reply. She writes something they said often in group: *Healing doesn't have a schedule.* Then she adds, *I don't appreciate you giving advice about something you don't know anything about.*

She takes the bottle of Celexa out of the medicine cabinet, like she does every morning, but this time she decides to put it back without taking one. She texts Olive about it. Sometimes she texts Olive when she is about to climb a ladder or take a bath, just in case she gets into an accident and no one finds her for days. She has never lived alone before and the feeling that she can just disappear still hasn't totally faded. *I just want to let you know, in case I have side effects or withdrawal or anything.*

You should taper, replies Olive.

If I do that, I'll just keep taking them. I need to be decisive.

She pours the capsules into the toilet and flushes. Then she worries about what it might do to the fish in Lake Ontario. She does what the anxiety books suggest in moments of worry—goes outside and moves her body. She puts Coach in the car and drives to Cherry Beach for a walk like she used to do when he was a puppy. She knows she'll end up carrying him, but she wants to be near the water, to look out and get a new perspective.

7

Gibson was asleep and now he is . . . having sex? Yes, this is happening, she's a real person, kissing his neck. He'd been dreaming about working on a conveyor belt sorting Christmas ornaments. He'd left Kelly and Julian's place, still kind of drunk and totally disoriented, and then he'd chugged coffee while touring the hospital ERs and gone home to fall asleep on the couch and wait for Cammie to call to clear things up, or to call the police to report her missing. And now here she is.

"Wait," he says, grabbing her hand away and sitting up. "Why didn't you call me back? You went to the hospital. I was so worried!"

"It's okay, they know me so well at the Western, it was like going back to work. They cleared me. Just a false alarm, but my oncologist said to take every pain seriously, you know? And I'm feeling better now, obviously." She takes off her dress and throws it across the room, grinning. He has to close his eyes to keep talking; he pulls himself up off the couch and tries to get his head straight. He *knows* she's lying. He feels it all over his body. He's never been more certain of an instinct.

"I called the hospital. They said you were never there."

Cammie's face goes blank for a beat. "You called the Western?"

"Of course. I was terrified for you. I even went in person! You weren't answering your phone. I didn't want you to be alone."

Cammie sits up and starts putting her dress back on. She avoids eye contact. He isn't sure how to interpret her behaviour. She's moving briskly, avoiding his eyes; she zips up her dress like she's mad at it. She's mad?

"Why are you mad that someone is concerned for you?"

She makes a sound like a huff, pulling up her socks and stuffing her feet in her boots, grabbing her purse.

"I told you I like to handle my medical shit alone. I don't need a caretaker. Why do you overstep boundaries? You're being so controlling."

He inhales deeply and counts to three in his head. She's standing by the window in a way that looks posed, effortful. The only thing you can see from the living room window is the red brick of the house next door. She's looking at it like it's a painting, all to avoid looking at him. He takes her purse from her hands and puts it down on the coffee table and grabs both her wrists.

"Cammie, come on. I can tell you're lying to me."

She makes a face like she's been punched. She takes her hands from his and crosses her arms.

"Uh, the reason they told you I wasn't there is because you probably asked for Camilla Parker, but that's not my legal name. Parker is my mother's maiden name. I started using it when I left home. But my OHIP card still says Wells."

The relief Gibson feels is immense. There is an explanation. Fucking Tess had worked him up, making him paranoid. This relief is short-lived, though, because embarrassment takes over. She's really looking at him now, as all the muscles in his face relax.

"Do you believe me?" she asks, sitting on the edge of the couch, pulling her knees up to her chest. "I mean, if you don't, I already have bruising from the IV." She points to her arm. He can't really see it, but he doesn't want her to feel bad.

"It really triggers me when people don't believe me. We have to trust each other if we're going to be in a relationship. Maybe we moved too quickly into this thing," she says.

Gibson panics. He's really fucked this up.

"I'm sorry, Cammie. I was worried. Then I was angry. I mean, imagine someone lying about that kind of thing—they'd have to be a monster. I know you're not a monster."

"It's okay, baby," she says, pulling him close. "I get it. You just jumped to conclusions."

"We're still getting to know each other, you know, we've moved really fast. Julian and Kelly kept saying that last night, and it's like I hadn't even noticed how fast because it just feels right."

"When it's right, it's right. Why waste time going slow when you finally find something magical? It's like, sometimes you meet the exact right person at the exact right time."

Gibson gets caught up in the tornado of this kind of magic talk until they're in bed, and then ordering Thai food from their favourite place, and then watching her favourite movie, *A League of Their Own,* and she talks along with the dialogue and he finds it so endearing. They've had their first big conflict and they are fine. Better than fine. Doesn't conflict ultimately bring people closer? It feels that way. He never had this with Veda. The extremes. They curl around each other on the couch and he doesn't want to be anywhere else. Her phone buzzes. He pauses the movie as she reads the text and then pumps her fist.

"My friend Shelby got me a job interview, on a TV show! Holy shit. This is my ticket out of service."

"That's awesome. Who's Shelby?"

"She's this older chick I met at the grief support group. She's a lesbian. I think she might have a crush on me, so she's not too keen on you."

"What? That's nuts."

Cammie shrugs and takes her phone into the bathroom.

He picks up his phone and scrolls Cammie's Instagram, which mostly consists of dogs she meets on the street and things she buys at yard sales in between thirst trap selfies. He looks for the name Shelby in her list of followers and finds a sparsely updated account of mostly memes about grief and photos of a pug. He scrolls far enough down to find a wedding photo with two women, a thin, athletic woman in a suit, and a bigger, feminine woman in a fairly casual white dress with big boobs and an average face. He keeps scrolling until he finds a selfie, confirming she is the feminine one. He feels a bit of relief about this, though he knows he shouldn't. He hears the bathroom door open and closes the app quickly.

"I'm so excited for this gig—it's a reality dating show."

"When's your interview?"

"Tomorrow at noon. Man, I'll be able to afford a great apartment."

"That is awesome, babe. I'm really happy for you."

"You don't mind if I keep staying here until then, though, right?"

"Are you kidding? I love having you here." That's true, but he does like the idea of her having her own place. Just so they don't have to act like they have moved in together so quickly.

"Okay, cool. Shelby is coming to pick me up and prep me for this gig. I'm going to crash with her tonight, but I'll be back tomorrow?"

"I can pick you up after your interview, if you like. Take you somewhere to celebrate?"

"I would love that. You're the best!"

After she leaves, Gibson tries to watch the end of the movie, but he goes back to social media and looks at all of Cammie's accounts. He can't stop himself. His inner monologue says he is just excited about a new crush, but underneath it he is still trying to prove Tess wrong. He'd immediately felt relief when Cammie had a plausible explanation for what the ER nurse had told him over the phone. But the relief was momentary and the feeling strongest when she was right in front of him. Something about her face, the way she looked at him, the way their bodies moved together in space. It was like being hypnotized. He believed her because to not believe her means something is wrong about how they seem to exist in space so beautifully together. It means something is wrong about how he feels deeply understood by another human for the first time in his life, that he has found someone who mirrors him so well it's almost uncanny.

He eats some leftover takeout, tries to read the novel he's been trying to read since the divorce, but once again goes back to his phone. He logs into Facebook and looks at her friends and family. He scrolls through all of her old photos, mostly from family parties, and with a few ex-boyfriends. Her account goes back years. He clicks on James's profile—indeed he was some kind of boxer or wrestler type. His posts are banal and misspelled, and Gibson wonders what on earth a smart girl like Cammie talked to him about. In photos they appear with cans of beer around a campfire, on ATVs out in the bush, at baseball games. He tries to remember when her friend Morgan would have died—she'd said it was during a citywide blackout. He remembers the year that happened and looks back at that time. Nothing. He searches the name Morgan, finds no one. He looks at last year's photos, when he imagines she would have been the sickest and in treatment, but finds no signs of anything like that. Just photos of her and Tommy at the Air Canada Centre watching a Heart concert; at Pride, where she appears tanned, healthy. You'd never have known she was sick. Did she really hide it that well? He googles the Arcade Fire record and her name, and nothing comes up. She has no photos from Los Angeles or Louisiana. The only photos outside Ontario appear to be in Montreal, in college, and a trip to Florida with her mother and sister. He clicks on the sister's profile—it's still active. But it's quite private. There are no memorial postings, no notices of her death. But the last public post is from five years ago. She appears to have been a paramedic in Simcoe. He clicks on her profile photo and finds it strange that no one has commented with heart or angel emojis, the way they normally do after someone dies. He googles her name + "obituary" and comes up with nothing.

He is losing his mind. Does he really think that she lied about going to the ER, and also lied about her sister dying? What kind of person would do that? And what kind of person would think that about someone he's falling in love with? He breaks out into a weird sweat and his heart rate speeds up. He wishes someone were there to talk this through with, but who could he talk to about this?

If he is truly this suspicious, he should just break up with her, call it a fling, and let it go. He takes a beer out onto the back deck and watches the squirrels in the trees. He misses his dog, who passed away last year. The dog really united him and Veda. He briefly misses Veda, too. He starts to text her *How you holding up?* But then he remembers the party and feels embarrassed.

He flips through Instagram again and up pops a photo of Shelby and Cammie, mugging for the camera. The caption shocks him: *When you meet the right person at the exact right time.*

He calls the Toronto Western Hospital and asks the nurse who answers if Camilla *Wells* has been discharged. He explains what time she'd have come in, how he is worried because of her recent cancer treatments, how she isn't picking up her phone. He is aware as he's speaking that he is lying as well. He can't remember the last time he lied to a stranger.

"No one checked in here by that name all weekend."

"Anyone else named Camilla? Maybe she used the name Parker?"

The nurse sighs. "No Camillas at all."

He hangs up the phone, despondent.

———

Tomorrow he'll pick Cammie up after her job interview and confront her. Though he just wants to go back a few days, before he felt any suspicion, and just pretend it's okay, keep having honeymoon sex and this new intense emotional intimacy. But he can't be in denial about having spent the whole evening as an amateur detective with a pit of anxiety in his stomach. He looks up the studio and plans his route.

He is prepared for every eventuality except the one that occurs.

8

A piece of buttered rye toast is always tasty. One bite can win you over, especially with a few ovals of a ripe banana, a spoonful of ricotta in a hopeful smear, some hemp hearts sprinkled on top of it all. There's something so comforting about toast at any time of day. Shelby stands in the bread aisle of Metro, imagining this future repast. Her appetite is returning, slowly and unpredictably, but for at least one meal a day. She selects a jar of honey, the most expensive one, which tells you where it was made. If the beehives are close to where you live it's supposed to help with seasonal allergens. She moves the loaf of rye bread over slightly, so that the honey doesn't squish it. Everything feels normal unless she moves her head quickly to one side. Then it's like her brain is zapped in a way that makes her aware her head is a skull and a skull is both the strongest, most important thing, but also vulnerable. This is a common side effect of going off SSRIs; she has a page of symptoms bookmarked on her phone. She's been taking one on occasion and then going a few days, and then taking it again in a moment of fear. But now she is committed. No more. She hates this feeling, but she also loves the feeling of not being medicated. She's just normal now. Raw. Like everyone else.

She moves on to the produce aisle, where she examines a green plastic basket of strawberries for freshness. She gently squeezes an English cucumber. She palms a head of iceberg lettuce, remembering that Cammie thinks it is the best lettuce, that what it lacks in nutrition it makes up for in crispness. She walks over to the cereal aisle and looks up a TikTok recipe video for lettuce wraps with a chickpea mixture inside. In the middle of the video she gets multiple texts from Melanie, Kate's sister. She doesn't respond to them. She knows what Melanie wants and she doesn't want to deal with it. She deletes the texts and watches the video again.

Shelby is less prone to panic attacks in the grocery store if she has something to focus on, like a recipe, a future plan. She puts a box of Cap'n Crunch into the last remaining spot in the basket. It's for Cammie. She spent the previous evening helping her prep for a job interview to be a production assistant on Olive's reality show. She lent her some professional clothes and drove her to the production office in the east end and dropped her off. She periodically checks her phone for texts, hoping it's going okay.

She is so absorbed in watching the recipe video on mute that she doesn't see Carol Jo from grief group in front of her until she feels a tug on her sleeve.

"Hey, lady," Carol Jo says. She has a silver mullet with a purple rat tail and appears to wear blue and purple Teva sandals all year round. She's holding a carton of eggs. For some reason she often smells like fresh earth, like she's just come in from the garden.

"Oh, hello."

Shelby's not sure what to say, so she holds up the cereal she's buying for Cammie. "I'm letting Cammie crash with me when she wants. She likes this kind."

"You seem really happy about that," Carol Jo says, with a warm smile.

"It's nice to come home to someone," she admits, tearing up and then wiping away the tears with her shirt sleeve.

"I told Nancy I wouldn't go on about this, but I just want to say that Cammie is a beautiful person, such a big heart, and I love that girl to bits. But she's always had trouble—trouble follows her around, and I just want to make sure that you have boundaries with her."

"Of course!" Shelby says. "Isn't it strange that her life is like a crazy movie? But yes, I mean, I'm the older one and I've been around the block. I know how to have boundaries."

"Good, good. You're a smart cookie. Cammie is a storyteller, you know, lots of melodrama. Sometimes people learn to be story-tellers as a survival strategy. I get the feeling that the worst stuff that happened to Cammie she would never actually talk about."

"Like, you think she has secrets? She's an open book!"

"We all grieve and cope in our own ways," Carol Jo says, open-ing up the egg carton and inspecting each individual egg. She does have what looks like dirt under her fingernails, and a tattoo of a labrys on her wrist that Shelby hasn't noticed before.

"Old school," Shelby says, pointing to her tattoo.

"Nancy has the same one."

"Kate had one on her ankle when she first came out, and then she covered it up with an illustration of her dog, but I think she regretted doing that."

"Herstory is important," Carol Jo says, so earnestly that Shelby just nods.

"So you think Cammie has secrets?" Shelby asks. She often has delayed reactions to things people say; she rarely has the right responses at the right time. "I mean, she knows how to keep you captivated with a story," Shelby says, unsure what Carol Jo was getting at.

"We're all complicated. Cammie's no different," she says, putting the eggs in her basket.

Months later, holed up in her closet with the dog, Shelby would remember this conversation and wish Carol Jo had been more explicit with her warnings.

When they part ways Shelby is suddenly aware of the brightness of the lights, the proximity of a child with a runny nose, a disconcerting vibration in the floor. She rushes to the checkout line, her only thought about leaving the building as quickly as possible. After placing the groceries in the back of the car, she sits in the driver's seat for two minutes, doing some deep breathing exercises before turning over the ignition.

———

When she gets home she unpacks the groceries, leaving the things she bought for Cammie out on the counter like a present. Then she goes down to the basement, which is the only part of the house that looks basically the same as it did before her parents moved out. Looking at it now, anticipating what Cammie might think of spending time there, she contemplates redecorating. When Shelby was a teenager it was her refuge. The thick, ugly white carpet was great for muffling the sound of late-night phone calls from her parents' eavesdropping. The brown plaid chesterfield that pulls out into a bed is the same as it ever was. She and Kate purchased a mattress pad to make it more comfortable for their guests, and they replaced Shelby's father's sports posters from the 1970s and '80s with tapestries they'd purchased from a women's arts and crafts exhibit, but otherwise the room is essentially the same.

There is a guest room on the second floor as well, in what used to be Shelby's childhood bedroom, but it is also an office and she feels like Cammie would appreciate having some privacy and her own bathroom.

On one side of the basement room is an area with a vinyl work-out bench and a small vertical shelf of hand weights, and on the other side is the couch against the far wall and the La-Z-Boy that their cat Binkie had ripped to shreds in the 1990s, propped in front of the old television and the VCR that was once her pride and joy and is now like an antique she can't part with. Beside the chest freezer, next to the washing machine and the furnace, are five Rubbermaid containers of Kate's belongings. Old photograph albums, sports equipment, camping gear, tax documents. She wasn't a pack rat the way Shelby is, but they were things she'd never unpacked or found a place for when they'd combined households.

The tiny en suite powder room has a bubble-gum-pink sink and a toilet with a wooden seat and is wallpapered with vintage issues of the *New Yorker*. There's a photo of her mother putting up the wallpaper in an old album. She wears a red handkerchief on her head and white bell-bottom jeans. Kate used to call it the swingers' bathroom. Shelby has been urged by friends to move Kate's things around, or out of the house, only when it really feels right. This is why she's not answering Melanie's texts.

She opens one of the Rubbermaids and the smell of Kate comes rushing at her and she closes it up and runs back up the stairs. She puts a leash on Coach and decides to take him out around the block. But when she opens the door she is greeted by Melanie, who looks like she has been standing on the porch debating whether to ring the doorbell.

"Hi," she says, and half smiles, looking worried. "I'm sorry to intrude. You never got back to me and I thought I would take a shot that you might be home."

Melanie is dressed like she's about to go to the gym, but her clothes are so pristine Shelby knows they aren't her actual workout clothes. She leans down to give Coach some belly rubs. Shelby doesn't quite know what to do. She hates it when anyone drops in, let alone someone whose nose from certain angles looks just like Kate's nose. Their hands look alike as well, she realizes, though Melanie's fingernails are long and oval and have tiny jewels on the thumbnail.

"No, no, it's fine. Come in," she says, backing into the front vestibule and unclipping Coach's leash. She kicks off her sandals as Coach jumps up onto the couch and makes a huffing sound. She offers Melanie a drink as she walks through the living room and into the kitchen. Melanie hovers, looking at the photos on the wall of their wedding, Pride photos, baby photos of their friends' kids, a group photo from a family reunion from Kate's side of the family.

"I've got mango juice, peach LaCroix, green tea, coffee, something stronger?"

"Tea sounds great," Melanie says.

Shelby plugs in the kettle and takes a sachet of green tea from the box. There's only one tea bag remaining after she uses this one. Kate bought the box. She decides not to offer it to anyone again and puts it in the back of the tea cupboard. She takes a clean mug out of the dishwasher and gives it a rinse in case there is any remaining residue from what she considers toxic dishwashing powder. This is something Kate used to mock her for that makes Shelby smile. She leans her head back out into the hall and sees that Melanie is still staring at the family reunion photo. For a moment it is nice to be with someone who remembers Kate.

"Do you want to keep it?" Shelby offers. She knows that's why Melanie is here. She wants things.

"Really?"

"Sure. Kate hated that photo. She was so hungover that day because it was Pride weekend, remember? I think she was still on molly. That was a few months before she got fully sober, don't know if you remember." Kate had detoxed and gone to rehab right when they first met, but she'd continued to use other drugs and drink on special occasions for a few years until giving up everything.

Melanie's face falls. It's so easy to forget that Kate's family has many *Live, Love, Laugh* and *Family Is Everything* decorative items but they also cannot handle any emotional communication that isn't positive, let alone admit the realities of life being a near-unending nightmare.

"Sorry," Shelby says, though she's not sure why she says it.

"No, it's fine. I'd love to take it."

She takes it off the tiny nail and slides it into her purse. There's a square of lighter paint beneath the frame. Suddenly Shelby regrets telling her she could take it. She hands her the tea and is about to suggest they sit on the front porch when Melanie asks if she can look at Kate's clothes. Shelby nods. She gets it. She spends a lot of time with Kate's clothes. But it also feels invasive. She won't let her take anything.

Melanie follows her upstairs and into the bedroom. Shelby slides the mirrored closet door open on Kate's side. Several pairs of jeans, immaculately hung, some white dress shirts; the majority of her clothes are an assortment of flannel shirts. There's a tie rack and a few suit jackets. Shelby hopes Melanie won't go pawing through the dresser drawers. She sits on the edge of the unmade bed as Melanie touches the shirts, as though looking for something in particular.

She doesn't want Melanie's perfume or hand cream to mix with the smells she's trying to preserve in Kate's side of the closet.

"I'm looking for a baseball shirt, from when she was a teenager. She used to wear it all the time. It's kind of old-fashioned-looking. You know the one, right?"

"Yeah, I know the one," Shelby says.

"I would really love to have it."

"Absolutely not," Shelby says before she thinks about why she's saying it. She's livid suddenly, standing up from the edge of the bed, in fight mode.

"Why? It reminds me of the best years of Kate and me as sisters. You know, we shared a bedroom, she used to lend it to me sometimes."

"No," Shelby says, "I can't let you have it. There's a tie-dyed Grateful Dead shirt from high school she kept for some reason. You can have that."

"No, I want the baseball shirt. Please. She was my sister."

"No."

"I don't understand. Why are you being like this?"

"Take one of her T-shirts, or work shirts, or ties," Shelby says, just trying to end the interaction.

"I don't want those things," she says.

"Why? They're all quintessentially Kate."

"This shirt is attached to a memory of a time before," she says. Melanie is flustered; she kneels down in front of the closet and starts opening up the drawers.

"Before what?"

"Before we were adults, before life was so serious."

"Oh, you mean before she was gay, before you guys were fucking weird with her?"

"That's not fair. It was a different time."

"I'm sorry, but no. Choose something else."

"I want that shirt."

Melanie starts frantically pawing through the closet now. Shelby tries to physically stop her. "Back off, it's not in there anyway."

"Where is it?"

"I don't know."

"You *do* know."

Shelby is suddenly fuelled by an intense annoyance, remembering all the stories Kate used to tell about her family being shitty to her when she came out. Melanie says she doesn't remember much but she fully benefited from being the preferred child for many years. Their parents paid for her college tuition, gave her a car. Kate left at sixteen and fended for herself entirely. Not only that but Shelby feels all the anger she's ever felt at straight people pretending they don't see or benefit from homophobia.

"It's in a box under the bed." She regrets saying this as soon as it's out of her mouth, but it feels like the quickest way to get rid of her.

Melanie looks confused by Shelby's sudden turnaround but kneels down to start looking there.

"Come on, Mel, just get out of my room," Shelby says, but she also kind of wants her to keep looking.

When Mel finds the box she opens it up and her face goes white, realizing she's opened a box filled mostly with vibrators and strap-ons, but also some lingerie and costumes, and the baseball shirt. Melanie drops it and runs from the room.

"What, are you uncomfortable? I told you not to look," Shelby says, following her out, down the stairs. She feels like pushing her down the remaining steps. Her hands are trembling as they reach the kitchen.

Melanie puts her tea in the kitchen sink and turns on the tap.

"I don't understand," she's mumbling, washing the cup like she's in *Macbeth*.

"It was *A League of Their Own* role play, if you must know."

Melanie makes a disgusted face as she puts the cup in the drainer and heads for the door.

"I didn't answer your fucking calls for a reason. I'm not ready to part with anything yet. I don't want to be invaded like this."

"You're a fucking psycho. She should have left you. You were so controlling all the time, with your goddamn anxiety disorder. You know it used to drive her crazy, right?"

"Get out of my house!" Shelby screams, and Coach rushes up to Melanie, barking at her. She leaves, slamming the door.

"Thanks, fighter," she says to Coach.

Shelby gets into bed, cuddles the dog, and doesn't leave until the next grief group.

9

Gibson and Cammie sit in the cab of his truck outside Bakerbots, where he's taken her to celebrate what she says felt like a successful job interview for the reality show. Cammie eats her ice cream cone, and he sips an iced coffee, preparing to launch into what he's been rehearsing all day in the bathroom mirror at work.

"I know you lied about going to the hospital," he says, staring ahead through the windshield at a cat sleeping on top of the blue Mazda in front of them. He doesn't want to glance sideways until he gets the next sentences out. "I called the hospital again, gave them both names. You were never there."

"It was probably a different charge nurse."

"Nope, same one."

"I can't believe you take the word of an overworked and underpaid stranger instead of the woman you claim to love."

She starts to cry. He grips the steering wheel, forcing himself to stay strong. He knows in his gut the tears are as real as her story. He's not sure if she knows she's being manipulative in the moment, but he knows that it is, without a doubt, the outcome.

"Why are you being like this?" Her cries become louder, gasping. He can see her shoulders moving in his periphery. The cat is now washing its face in a beam of sunlight and then stops, alarmed by the sounds she's making.

"Show me your OHIP card. I want to see what name is on it," he demands, but his voice cracks. He can feel his resolve faltering.

"I don't have it with me," she says.

"You took your wallet out before," he says. He knows she has it because she got it out to fake-offer to pay for the ice cream. She sighs and pulls it out and throws it on his lap. It falls to the floor under the gas pedal. When he bends down to pick it up he wonders if she'll bolt from the truck. But when he sits back up and opens up her pink leather billfold, he turns to look at her and she's completely surrendered. No tears. Just staring ahead, and then at him, eyes empty.

There it is, Camilla Parker. A photo where she has straight, blunt bangs and looks younger. He has caught her. Her face burns red and she begins to eat her ice cream and stare into space. She looks young, like a daydreamy little kid who doesn't know what she's done.

"Okay, I lied," she whispers.

Gibson's entire body floods with adrenaline. Finally he has an actual answer, an admission. His hands began to tingle and he worries he's going to have a literal heart attack.

"Why? Why would you do that?"

"I was mad you didn't defend me in front of your friends. You didn't defend me to Tess. Then Veda got there and she's so pretty! And I did feel sick, and I was worried it was the cancer returning. I just decided not to go to the hospital."

"So you were jealous and so you made up being sick?"

"How dare you say I made up being sick?"

"Um, you just said you lied."

"No, I was going to go to the hospital because I *was* feeling sick, but I got so tired and I actually fell asleep in my apartment hallway, that's how sick I felt. When I woke up I felt better."

"Why not just tell me that?"

"I don't know why I said that. I'm sorry." She starts to cry again, heaving and sobbing and clinging to him.

He watches her cry, turning toward her but still gripping the steering wheel. What is the right thing to do in this situation? He hates to see her crying. He hates that he hurt her, even though he knows he should be the angry one.

It feels involuntary when he reaches over to pet her hair, even though he still feels angry. Then he consoles her, even though the gesture of consolation, the hand on her hair, feels confusing to him. He's still angry, but he also wants to understand.

"Lying is a big deal to me. I can't believe you lied about something so serious."

"I'm sorry, I'm so sorry, please don't leave me. I panic when I start to fall in love with someone, please don't leave," she wails.

"Shhh, shhh," he whispers as he holds her, feeling so many conflicting emotions. She looks so fragile. The anger that was so intense just moments ago is now shifting to sympathy. He grasps for anything to say that might make the situation feel less melodramatic or unusual.

"Why don't we go see a counsellor together, maybe try to figure out how to communicate better?" He hears himself say it before it makes any logical sense. Everyone has bad habits. Maybe lying when she doesn't get her way or needs attention is hers. The important thing is to acknowledge it and work on it not happening again. Now everything is out in the open. Couldn't it change?

"Yes, I'll do anything, anything. I'll make it up to you, I promise." She starts to kiss him and then straddles him, and as they kiss he feels even more confused and weird and unsettled but he can't stop making out with her.

———————

A few weeks later Gibson goes to his annual physical. His blood pressure is high for the first time in his life and he has to confess several things. He hasn't been sleeping much. He's been drinking more. He's been driving too much and walking too little. His doctor asks about history of heart disease in the family and says he should probably lay off the red meat, get back to the gym. Gibson admits he is stressed out all the time, though on paper things are actually okay. He leaves with a referral for a therapist that he crumples up and drops in his truck's cup holder.

After his physical he goes to get blood taken at a lab. He pops in his earphones because he can't stand the sound of the needle and vials, and he looks at a stain on the ceiling tile above the cubicle as the nurse draws his blood. He always feels too tall, too awkward for the tiny little space and the chair with the armrest, which he suspects is not sterilized between people like it is in a tattoo shop. He feels the whirring awareness of a potential migraine behind his eyes. Why is he so stressed out? His work is going well. Tina decided she wasn't going to quit after all. He can get everything done in about four hours and for the other four he takes leisurely lunches and plays video games and fakes work. The devastation of the divorce has stopped being so acute. He's in love with Cammie and has hopes about mending a friendship with Veda. He hasn't seen his friends much, but everyone's been busy. And maybe he's been avoiding Julian. The last time they'd met for a beer he left early, feigning a headache. But the truth is, he left because Julian had made an offhand comment about Cammie. "Something is always *up* with her. It's like she never has a week without some calamity befalling her. There's so much drama!" Ever since then he can't shake a type of ambient anxiety. And every time there is something new in Cammie's life that goes wrong, he hears Julian's mocking tone of voice in his head. He's become adept at trying to fix everything for Cammie. She asks him not to, mostly, but then takes him up on things. Like paying her landlord the back rent she'd owed so her credit wouldn't go in the garbage.

When the nurse presses a piece of gauze to his arm and then tapes it down, he thanks her and stands up too quickly, getting light-headed, and has to sit back down. He doesn't like feeling unstable or physically weak. He blushes and gets up again, putting on his jacket quickly and stumbling clumsily out of the lab and into the hospital corridor. He stops at Second Cup and buys a muffin and a bottle of water. He is drinking too much coffee and not eating enough, he surmises.

Couples therapy with Cammie was a disaster. Cammie told a middle-aged mom-like therapist all about her alcoholic father, the death of Morgan, and her sister. The therapist was clearly in love with her. She barely asked Gibson a question. When he did speak, he felt like she was judging him. Toward the end of the session he said, "We're here because Cammie lied to me about being sick and going to the hospital. There's some broken trust." She gave him a line about how she had to get to know them both first, their traumas and families of origin, and therapy wasn't like going to a garage to get a tune-up. He felt belittled in that moment. When they left, Cammie was smiling; she said she felt like the therapist was solid, would be good for them. He paid for it and then booked another session, but he doesn't want to go. There wasn't a single moment in the session where he felt like Cammie took responsibility for what had happened, or even acknowledged it. He felt like he had watched her manipulate the therapist into being on her side.

But then they had a bit of a honeymoon period after that. They went to Niagara Falls and did mushrooms and went go-karting and stayed in a crazy hotel room with a heart-shaped tub. Life with Cammie was extreme in its ups and downs, and Gibson had to admit it was exciting still; the ups were higher than he'd ever experienced and he felt like they were almost worth the corresponding crashes.

But he has started to realize that the days Cammie spends at Shelby's are calmer. He's able to rest more, eat better, and just generally feel more on top of his life when it's just him in the apartment. He misses Cammie; he reaches for her in bed when she isn't there. And he likes the way she keeps everything spotless and brings him home treats every time she leaves the house. But there is a quiet he yearns for when she spends too much time at his place. And while their relationship started out as a love fest, she's begun to get impatient with him, snapping at him in unpredictable ways, saying offhand cruel things about his weight, his age. She apologizes, but always in a weird way that makes him feel like he doesn't understand what's happening. He's noticed that if he feels she isn't being honest with him, and he lets on in some way, she either turns it around on him, distracts him with sex, or tells him he is the most sensitive man she's ever met and that it turns her off.

When they make up, though, it's like a honeymoon again, passionate and frenzied, and in those moments it's like he can't remember feeling any other way besides head over heels.

When he gets home from the doctor's Cammie calls and says Shelby has invited them both over for dinner the next day. He's into it. The more he knows other people in Cammie's life, the more they will feel like a real couple and not just some random, dramatic affair.

10

When Gibson knocks on the door, Shelby is stirring cherry tomatoes in olive oil, watching them blister in the heat, singing along to Jason Isbell. She calls Cammie's name and looks over at the door to the basement, where Cammie went to do laundry half an hour ago. She presses a wooden spoon down on a tomato, watches it burst.

Shelby has been trying to keep an open mind about Gibson, but it's been a bit difficult. That week Cammie shared with the group that she was still preoccupied with her ex-boss, who was smearing her reputation, and that her old friends were taking the boss's side and it wasn't fair. She was bereft to lose her closest friend, Tommy, who had been her work husband and was believing the bad boss instead of Cammie. It was triggering the memories of having lost Morgan. Her old boss wasn't paying her money owed for work she'd done in the last week. She'd lent what little she had to Gibson, who was apparently a gambler, she'd only recently discovered. She'd begged him to go to couples therapy and they had just had their first appointment. Shelby hasn't yet heard how it went.

The doorbell rings. This time Coach Taylor goes wild, yapping and wriggling his butt, unused to hearing the doorbell lately. As she wipes her hands on her apron, she calls Cammie again. She approaches the front door and suddenly feels quite nervous and regrets inviting Gibson, like she doesn't have the energy for this interaction. This is what happens lately: she makes a plan a week away and then when the day arrives she has no will to follow through. She's worried about Gibson, how awkward this dinner might be. Cammie hasn't always said the nicest things about him. Shelby is using this opportunity to get a vibe from him, make sure he's okay. A great thing about being gay is never really having to interact with unsavoury men inside your own house.

The man on the front step is sweet-faced and grinning, clutching a good wine and a bouquet of lillies. "You must be Shelby," he says. He wears an outfit like Kate might have, soft blue-and-green plaid, jeans that could be from any era. When she shakes his hand it is soft.

"The famous Gibson," she replies, just like her mother would have, taking the flowers and stepping aside to let him in. He removes his sneakers, though she tells him he doesn't have to. She brings him into the kitchen and roots around to find a vase, settling on an old pasta sauce jar she hasn't recycled yet.

"Your house is so lovely. I can see why Cammie likes it here," he says, accepting a glass of wine.

"Thank you," she says. "I hope you like pasta?"

"Who doesn't? I mean, it's basically nature's delicious sedative." He laughs nervously.

Shelby sees then that she's not the only one feeling a bit trepidatious about the evening. She raises her own glass in the air. "Cheers, Gibson. It's nice to finally meet you."

"Yes, cheers. So where's our girl?"

"You know, she's downstairs, if you want to go grab her."

She motions toward the door to the basement.

"Sure, sure." He puts his glass down on the kitchen table and goes downstairs.

———

Since Kate's sister's devastating drop-in, dead people group has become Shelby's lifeline. She's no longer the new girl; she's able to be supportive to the newer members who are still in shock and barely able to function. She *is* officially now able to function, go to work, do the habits of life. Mostly, anyway. She still isn't sleeping through the night. She washes her hair maybe twice per week. She cries every day. But she isn't sitting on the couch paralyzed, only getting up to care for Coach Taylor's basic needs. In fact, she's thinking of rescuing another dog so Coach won't be lonely when she goes out.

During her shares in group Shelby has told everyone about how Kate taught her to express her emotions, to name them and allow them to be in the room with them, instead of being passive-aggressive like her mother, or mutely in denial like her dad. She'd changed Shelby for the better. And she knows, despite what Melanie said, that she nurtured the same in Kate. After Melanie left she went back and read emails and messages from Kate confirming as much. *You've taught me to see the beauty in the world, and in myself,* Kate wrote to her in their last anniversary card. Shelby told the group about how they were planning to have kids, to maybe move to Arizona, where Kate wanted to start an artists' retreat. It feels like Kate can be present in the room with the group in a way she can't be among those who can't acknowledge death for what it is, who are always just quietly hoping Shelby will shut up about it. People like her mother.

Cammie always asks her questions about Kate. She never stops her or changes the subject when she talks about Kate. And she remembers things like how Shelby takes her coffee, and how she watches *Jeopardy!* every day because Kate always watched *Jeopardy!* and it makes her feel connected to her.

That Cammie is the one so many group members focus on doesn't bother her. Shelby prefers to be present but not in the spotlight, whereas Cammie always wants eyes on her. Nancy and Carol Jo, who have been going to the group for as long as it's existed, sometimes bring gifts for Cammie, like handmade mittens, snacks. Cammie confessed that Carol Jo once lent her money to pay for her cellphone when she was really broke, like she was Carol Jo's wayward daughter. Sometimes Shelby thinks the women at group act motherly toward Cammie in a weird, misplaced way because they've lost children themselves, but then she realizes she also does that sometimes, sort of. Focusing on Cammie and her many problems is a way to ignore her own. But it feels too good to stop doing it.

———

Gibson comes back upstairs without Cammie. "She's just taking a minute to get dressed," he says, though his face is flushed and Shelby wonders if they've been fighting.

As she dresses the salad and asks Gibson to slice up a lemon and some fresh chives, she tells him that having Cammie around has been helpful to her. "She keeps me from getting too eccentric in my grief, you know? Her friendship feels like friendships did back in high school, like we never small talk. She listens really well. We never hide our feelings," she says.

"I feel that way too. When I first started spending time with her I started wondering if my friends were as courteous and loyal as I'd been assuming, you know? She's really uniquely generous," he says.

"Cammie puts in the work to really get to know someone. She's quite special. You're very lucky," she says.

"Oh, I know. She's really changed my life too," he says. He gives her a bit of a strange look and then asks if she has a girlfriend. She knows why he's asking.

"No, I'm not ready to date yet. I can't imagine ever having feelings. For anyone," she says, leaving the *Don't worry about me stealing your girl* silent.

"Cammie seems to have done great work on the reality show," Shelby says. "Olive told me that everyone loved her."

"Yeah, I heard the wrap party was fun," he says, putting the finished salad on the table.

"Yeah, it was," she says. She hadn't been sure why Cammie had invited her and not Gibson, but when she got there she realized it might be because a lot of the group were queer. A cute andro girl called Maude tried to flirt with Shelby and she got so flustered by it, and the idea that she would ever move on from Kate, that she went home early. She cried in the car, wondering if she'd ever have sex again, or even just have feelings like she'd want to kiss someone again. Sometimes it feels like that part of her died with Kate.

"Anyway, Olive is looking out for her, you know, for a next job. That's kind of how it works in TV, apparently."

By the time Cammie emerges, Shelby feels completely relaxed with Gibson. Kate would have said that he had good vibes. Calm, not an overtalker, but not too quiet either. Cammie gives him an awkward kiss, but eventually their dynamic evens out. Shelby sets the dining room table and they have a proper dinner, the way she hasn't all year.

Gibson turns out to be a fairly innocuous guy. Closer in age to her than Cammie, a typical Southern Ontario type who likes video games and has an entirely forgettable job and some good memories of seeing the Tragically Hip one summer. He has some gay friends, so any fears she had about him being a bit redneck were unfounded. Most of all, Shelby doesn't pick up toxic dynamics between him and Cammie. He speaks to her kindly, almost as if he were a respectful fan and not her boyfriend. When she goes to the bathroom Shelby gives him the line from every rom-com about not messing with Cammie. You mess with the bull, you get the horns. He gives her a big-eyed and innocent look, as though she didn't know about the gambling, the potentially sketchy reasons why Cammie sometimes shows up late at night. Maybe he has problems, but doesn't everyone? She doesn't see any red flags at all.

He helps to light the barbecue so they can roast bananas and caramel in tinfoil for dessert. He tells delightful stories about his childhood, and when they hug goodbye he gives her a tight squeeze and thanks her for taking such good care "of our girl." After they go home she texts Cammie that he seems like a good guy. To hold on to him, because he seems solid. Cammie doesn't answer the text and Shelby worries she's shot herself in the foot—of course, any guy can put on a good show. She follows it up with *But of course you know him better than I do. I trust your opinions and feelings!*

Now she seems crazy. She puts her phone away.

————

When she gets home from work the next day she almost doesn't notice that anything is amiss. She thinks perhaps she forgot to lock the door and it swayed open in the wind. Mercifully the dog is asleep in the bedroom, unfussed. The living room looks almost normal, but the kitchen cabinets are open. It's hard to put her finger on it but she realizes things have been moved around—the fruit bowl is on the counter, not the table. The pad of paper and cup of pens she keeps on the small table between the living room and kitchen is on the floor. Her candlesticks have been knocked over; the throw blanket Shelby compulsively refolds and places neatly on the couch is strewn on the coffee table. In her bedroom, her dresser drawers are emptied out, her jewellry missing from the box. Her laptop is gone.

She calls the police. She's never had to call the police before and when they arrive they look ten years younger than her and not at all strong or mighty. They sit at her kitchen table looking like guys she went to high school with. *Everything is fake,* she thinks. *The systems in place to protect us. Money is fake. All of it.* She answers their questions while in a weird existential funk. Maybe she should just get rid of all her possessions. Maybe she's been unburdened.

"Does anyone have a key?" the taller one asks, taking notes in a flip-top notebook.

"Just the friend staying downstairs," Shelby says.

"And what's her name?"

"Camilla Parker," she says. And then it occurs to her. "But her boyfriend is a gambler. He just came over for dinner, actually."

"Ah," they say knowingly, like this is the answer. "Did he look around the house much when he was here?"

"Well, I gave him a tour, I guess."

She gives them Gibson's name and address and sits on her front porch with the dog, surveying the street and texting with her dad and Olive, who both say she should change the locks. She calls an emergency locksmith, who is there within the hour. Her dad goes to Home Depot to get a security monitoring system and a sensor light. She watches him install everything from the porch, shaken that she was so wrong about Gibson. Has she lost the ability to judge character? She feels bad for not trusting Cammie when she wanted to keep them apart. She wants Cammie to break up with him immediately and texts her as much, demanding she come home, where it is safer.

Her dad offers to stay the night; they can watch hockey and order pizza. It's a sweet offer but she needs to be alone, so she declines, promising to call if she needs anything. Her parents' condo is only a few kilometres away.

———————

Shortly after Shelby's dad leaves, Cammie shows up at the back door. Shelby hears her try the keys and be thwarted by the new locks. Shelby opens the door. Cammie is snapping her gum, looking impatient and angry.

"Hey, my key's not fucking working."

"I'm so glad you're here. You need to leave Gibson."

"Why did you give the police his name? I can't believe you!" she screams. "He's a dangerous man!"

She barges into the kitchen and walks right through to the living room sofa, where she collapses on her back like a teenager.

"Uh, does that mean you think he robbed me? Why would you be with someone who would do that?"

Cammie pauses, then pivots her position.

"I don't know, I don't think he would steal from someone he knows."

"You just said he was dangerous! He didn't seem dangerous to me, but sometimes sociopaths are very clever. But that wasn't the vibe I got. Maybe it was just bad timing that someone broke in right after he was here."

"You don't know him like I do. He's complicated."

"If he's so dangerous, why do you stay with him?"

"I guess I have a type."

"Did the cops take him in?"

"No, they didn't have any evidence, but he got really freaked out."

Shelby notices she has a bandage on her arm. "Did he hurt you?"

Cammie pauses as though deciding on her answer.

"No, I got a new tattoo. Look, if you don't mind, I just really need to be alone and go to sleep," she says, standing up and going down into the basement.

Shelby feels uneasy. Something isn't right but she can't put her finger on it. She goes outside on the porch again, trying to calm down. She places her hand on her chest like her therapist told her to do. Then she goes on Facebook on her phone and accepts the friend request from Gibson that he sent the night before. If he is mad about the cops showing up at his door, he'll unfriend her. She scrolls through years of his feed, his incredibly average, mostly boring feed. He had a wife until very recently. He went to Oktoberfest. He has cottage photos, grandparent photos. He mostly seems like the straight male version of her. There are no photos at casinos, no flashy purchases, no bragging of any sort.

Shelby goes back inside, and as she takes off her shoes she notices that Cammie's trademark scuffed and aging white cowboy boots have been replaced by a shiny pair. Brand new. She notes the brand and looks up the cost—$800. Then she gets a text from Olive. *I hope you're not mad about the payday screwup for Cammie. Rest assured I couriered a cheque to her this evening.*

She feels deeply unsettled. And then a sudden, very certain realization: Cammie is the thief. She was the thief at her old job and that's why she was fired. That's why Tommy stopped being her friend. And now she has stolen from Shelby. What else was a lie?

Shelby grabs Coach Taylor and gets in her car and drives to Gibson's house.

11

When things with Cammie are going well, Gibson feels like a champion. This is how he feels while waiting in the car for Cammie after their dinner at Shelby's. She's gone back inside to get some clothes she's forgotten. The night is warm and lovely, and he leans his head back and hears the sound of kids playing ball hockey in the street a few yards down. The moon is full. The air is getting thicker with the smell of campfire from not too far away. He scrolls through Airbnb on his phone, looking for cabins free that weekend. A campfire. A walk in the woods. Jumping off cliffs into a lake? The weather has stayed summertime warm still. Maybe Shelby would like to come?

He's relieved to finally have met her, after he'd pleaded so many times to do so. He could never figure out why Cammie had made such a big deal about it. She'd met every single one of his friends, after all. He was extra nervous to meet Shelby, given all the buildup, and he overdid it by bringing a giant bouquet and expensive wine, and insisting on washing every dish so she'd know he wasn't the kind of guy who lets women do all the work. She lives on a quiet street in the Annex. He had been dying to ask how she afforded a house in such an expensive neighbourhood but couldn't figure out how to bring it up. She ended up admitting that her parents had owned it and they'd moved into a condo to downsize and left it to her. She kept staring at him like she wanted to ask him things too. All in all, he thinks the evening was a success. He feels happy to know Shelby, especially since she seems to take care of Cammie, like a sister figure. She is absolutely nothing like Cammie described.

When Cammie gets back in the car, he babbles to her about going away that weekend, but she's icy with him. He pulls out of the parking spot and she snaps, "Wait, I'm not buckled in yet!"

"Sorry," he says, pausing until he hears the seatbelt click.

"You tired, babe?" he asks a few minutes later as he pulls up to the lights at Bathurst and Bloor.

"Nope," she says. He gets a sinking feeling. He knows this tone of voice. Things are not okay.

"Shelby is so great! I really love her. I'm so glad to have met her finally. She's so different from how you described. Like, she's not a militant man-hater at all! I don't know why you told me that," he says.

"I didn't say that. Why are you putting words in my mouth?"

"You told me she doesn't like men and wouldn't like me. I remember those words specifically."

Cammie makes a sound like a scoff. He knows he shouldn't press but he wants to get to the bottom of it.

"You said she was controlling, like your sister, and you'd missed that dynamic, remember? But I don't know, she seems almost like a submissive person. Like she'd do anything for you!"

He'd pictured someone with a mean sneer, a sharp wit, judgmental. But she'd pulled him in for a hug when he arrived and she smelled like peaches and made sure he wasn't allergic to anything and that he liked the food and was comfortable. All through dinner

he was confused, the more Shelby talked. She didn't seem posses-
sive at all. She talked about how she wished she could date again
but wasn't sure she ever would. She didn't seem like a threat to
him in the slightest. In fact, she seemed almost maternal toward
Cammie. They have a shorthand, a series of inside jokes, just the
way he and Cammie do. He started to fantasize about them being
a trio of friends, going on group hikes and having a beer after
work. He liked her. He was pleasantly surprised. She seemed to
like him a lot too. Their shared love for Cammie bonded them. He
could see them becoming friends. He realized that was what he
wanted, to be a part of Cammie's whole life, not just the life
between them in his apartment, not just the sex or the romantic
dinners and comfortable Saturday afternoons.

"I'm just glad to meet her. She's important to you. You're important to me. It makes sense. I mean, soon we'll meet each other's
families, right?" He's asked to meet her mom, but Cammie said
she doesn't leave Owen Sound much. They've planned a few weekend trips up to meet her that have always fallen through at the last
minute. Meeting Shelby felt like he was really Cammie's partner
and that he was getting to see a side of her that he doesn't have
access to on his own.

Cammie pouts almost all the way home. He feels like he is waiting for her to explode, and he does what he did as a child when his
mother was in a mood—chatters about nothing, hoping to distract
her. He talks about how much he likes Shelby, how sad it is that
she lost her wife, how openly she talks about her panic disorder.

"She's brave," he says.

"Oh yeah, well, she hated you," Cammie says, inexplicably, putting her bare feet up on the dash. Gibson is shocked by this, feels
that childlike shame reminiscent of grade school, of not being
liked.

"How do you know? I really didn't get that vibe."

"She told me when you went to the bathroom."

He knows immediately that this is an absolute lie. No question. He's got a good read on people. It's how he's advanced so far at his job. And he's also developed a razor-sharp instinct about when Cammie is lying.

"Tell me exactly what she said," he demands. "What is it about me?"

She shrugs. A cyclist zooms by on his left and scares the crap out of him. He takes a deep breath.

"Cammie, are you jealous that Shelby and I might become friends?"

"That will never, ever happen."

"Were we at the same dinner? I thought we got along great. Why don't you want your friends to be friends with each other?"

"That's an insane accusation! And pretty rich, seeing as you seem fine with the fact that *your* friends don't like *me* because they think I'm a *liar*. You haven't even done anything to defend me to them, right?"

"Yes, I have." He tries to keep his voice calm and even, to not rise to the hysteria she is heading toward.

"So rich that they think I'm a liar when you just lied to my face right now."

"I have talked to them about it," Gibson says. "Obviously I wouldn't do it in front of you. I wouldn't want them to hurt your feelings."

"No wonder Veda dumped you. You're so weak. You can't even stand up for me for real, in front of me."

She monologues the rest of the way home, angrily. Her words almost don't make sense; it's like a wall of noise. Gibson finds it hard to pay attention to the road. He stops answering her, hoping she'll tire herself out. He can't find a parking spot in the area where he has a permit, and so he drops her off to go in and drives around in circles until he finally finds one two blocks away. The walk starts to clear his head but as he gets closer to the apartment he feels suffocated by the idea of resuming their fight.

He hears the shower running when he gets inside. He goes out to the back porch to calm down. With every fight they've ever had, he usually ends up feeling guilty but also confused. If he were to call a friend to describe the fight, he wouldn't be able to put into words what she'd said, or how he'd responded, or the order of things as they'd happened; it would be like trying to recount a fuzzy dream. He wishes sometimes he could record them and reflect later. Is it true that he isn't loyal to Cammie? He feels like his whole life these days actually revolves around her. He didn't even show up to Kelly's birthday because he didn't want to not invite Cammie to the dinner. She is so good at fighting, she can make him feel like a withering flint of nothing. But isn't arguing supposed to be good for a relationship? He and Veda rarely fought. When they disagreed and had to talk about it, it generally brought them closer. Gibson hates conflict. He is terrible at fighting. He apologizes often just to get things to stop being so loud or intense.

But this time he is pretty sure he hasn't done anything wrong. It's true he hasn't always been the most self-aware guy on earth. It's true that Veda insisted they see a couples therapist so that he could learn to communicate his feelings, and when he tries he is still really quite bad at it. But he thought he'd learned a thing or two since then. When he opens his phone his hands are shaking. He looks Shelby up on Facebook and clicks "Add Friend." If she really doesn't like him, she won't accept. Simple enough.

He gets into bed and turns on a movie he's watched a thousand times and falls asleep. He wakes up briefly sometime later when Cammie gets into bed. He expects she'll come on to him like she usually does after they've fought, but she doesn't. She turns to the wall and he can feel the heat of her silent anger just radiating off her.

———————

When he wakes up Cammie is already gone. She doesn't come home in the evening either and he assumes she's at Shelby's, which is almost a relief. He has felt off all day, couldn't concentrate on anything. He is dozing off in front of the seven P.M. *Law & Order* when he hears a banging on the front door, so loud he's afraid that the house is on fire and a neighbour is warning him to get out. But it's the cops, asking for him by name.

"Yes, that's me. Can I help you?"

It goes downhill from there.

"We just need to ask you a few questions. Can we come in?"

"Is everyone okay? Is it Veda? Has there been an accident?"

"No, no, we just have some questions about your whereabouts today. Can we come in?"

Every episode of *Law and Order* spirals in his mind. Did he do something wrong? Do they think he did something wrong? He breaks into a sweat and opens the door wider, ushers them up the stairs to the kitchen. He isn't guilty of anything, though, so why is he scared?

"Would you like water, a coffee?" he offers. He stands at the kitchen counter feeling helpless and confused.

"Why don't you sit down?"

"Sure, okay." He only has two kitchen chairs. He sits down across from the cop with the notebook. The other guy stands.

"Do you know Shelby Roberston?"

"Yes, we met last night. She's my girlfriend's good friend. Is she okay?"

"Yes, she's fine. She's just had a break-in. Do you have a gambling problem?"

"No, no, I don't. Why? Does she think I broke into her house?" They don't answer him. "I don't even buy lottery tickets. I went to a casino once with my buddies and got bored." Is he protesting too much? Does he sound like a liar?

The cop with the notebook writes something down.

"Where were you today?"

"I went to work, got home around six."

"Did you leave at any point during the day, for a lunch break?"

"Yeah, I went to a café across the street from the office."

"Can anyone vouch for you?"

"Sure. You can call my boss. I mean, I wish you wouldn't, for obvious reasons, but she'd be able to back that up. I mean, I have a receipt for my sandwich." He fishes around in his pocket and pulls it out. He gives the cop a business card, writes his boss's name and extension on the back of it. The cops start to look bored.

"Do you mind if we look around?"

This is the moment in *Law & Order* where the person usually says no to this request if they're guilty, so he just nods and says, "Go ahead. I have nothing to hide. I certainly didn't steal anything. I have money." He watches them move around, opening drawers in his filing cabinet, his dresser drawers, the file boxes in his closet he has yet to organize. After a while they stop.

"You don't have much stuff for a guy your age."

"I just got divorced. I gave her most of the stuff. I haven't done a lot of shopping."

The notebook cop shuts his pad and clicks his pen. "I been there."

"We'll be in touch, so answer your phone if we call, okay?"

"Okay," Gibson says. They start down the stairs just as Cammie comes in the front entrance.

"Oh my, what's going on? Everything okay?"

They ask her where she was all day and she tells them work, though Gibson knows she wasn't. She is charming and weirdly flirty with the cops. He watches them interact and it dawns on him that something is afoot. They stand at the bedroom window and watch the cops drive away and don't speak until they are out of sight. Cammie walks into the kitchen and starts rummaging around in the fridge like nothing is weird.

"Okay, can you explain, please?" Gibson asks.

"Well, someone broke into Shelby's house. I don't know why she would rat on you like that. I think she might be having a nervous breakdown, to be honest. She has serious mental health issues," Cammie says, sounding furious at Shelby as she cleans the kitchen. Gibson sits at the table, watching.

"Rat on me? Cammie, I didn't do anything. I'm not a thief. I have money. And Shelby's very open about her anxiety. I don't think she's crazy in the, like, classical sense."

"Why do you love her so much? You just met her. Believe me, she doesn't like you."

Gibson takes a breath. He doesn't want to keep engaging in a debate with her; it always goes off the rails. He looks at her and realizes several things all at once: She's been complaining about money for weeks. He's been paying for everything while she's been waiting for her first TV cheque. And now she stands in front of him in brand-new boots, with a new tattoo, and her hair looks shiny and big, like she's had a blowout. He understands what that means right away. He's about to accuse her but decides against it.

"You look great, babe. Did you go shopping?" He tries to make his voice neutral and normal, but his heart is racing, his entire chest pumping with adrenaline. He resents that her behaviour is making him behave in a manipulative, dishonest way. Cammie is a psychopath. He knows it at that very moment with everything inside him.

"Yeah, I got my cheque today," she says. Her voice shifts too, the rage evaporating and the familiar sex-kitten purr emerging as she gets close to him.

"That's weird—it came by courier today," he says, handing her the FedEx envelope.

"Well, I spent my savings. I'm going to use this to pay bills," she says.

She kisses him in a way he knows is about getting him to shut up, and he can't kiss her back. He makes his lips flat and pulls his head away.

"You told me you were broke. You couldn't even pay for the subway."

"Yeah, 'cause I left my bank card at the bar. I went back to get it and I had a few hundred bucks left from the last week of tip-outs."

She is lying. He is watching her improvise and lie right in front of him. He is astounded, even as he realizes that this makes every-thing that has happened previously in their relationship make sense.

"I bought you something," she says, reaching into her bag and pulling out a bottle of whiskey. A top-shelf brand. "I thought you deserved something special."

"Thank you," he says, knowing instantly that she swiped it from the bar.

"Let's have a drink and take off our clothes," she says, smiling mischievously as if they haven't fought at all, as if the cops haven't just left, as if he isn't totally on to her and she doesn't know it. But of course she does.

"Uh, I forgot, babe, I have to go to Julian's tonight. I told him I'd help him with his deck. Fuck, I can't believe I forgot." He is a bad liar. He sounds like a kid in a school play. But she can't call him on it.

He doesn't want her in the house by herself. He told her about the emergency credit card in the freezer, and he doesn't lock the drawer in his desk with all his tax information. He does a mental sweep of the place, remembering where anything valuable is. He knows confronting her won't work; she has an answer for everything. She opens the fridge and takes out a beer.

"Your loss."

He doesn't move. He isn't sure how to get her out of the apartment in a way that makes sense. Can he say *I'd like you to leave my house* without it becoming a thing? He is suddenly overwhelmed with the idea of how she might tell future stories about him, about their relationship. He thinks about how she described her ex as violent. He imagines his life ruined. Her phone sits on the kitchen table, blowing up with texts and calls from Shelby.

"Why aren't you picking up?"

"Uh, because she thinks my boyfriend is a thief. Fuck her."

"Why don't you go confront her about it? I mean, she seems otherwise reasonable. You can explain that it was just bad timing, that it was a stranger who robbed her. I mean, why would she think I'm a gambler?"

Checkmate. She doesn't have an immediate answer. He knows she must be the reason Shelby suspected him. He can see her brain moving, but finally it's not fast enough, so he continues.

"I'll drive you over on my way to Julian's."

"It's not on the way," she says, but she follows him out the door anyway. "And I'm not good at confrontation."

He laughs at that. "You are a great fighter, Cammie. The best I've ever witnessed. I can come in with you, if you like. We can both explain together that we had nothing to do with it."

Her face absolutely pales. This is what she looks like when she gets caught in a lie. Finally he's caught her for real and knows not to fall for her lies or her tears or sex. Her eyes look empty. Like she is looking at nothing and has nothing in her head.

"No, I'll do it myself," she says, quietly.

They don't speak on the drive there. But the air in the car pulses with the knowledge of her dishonesty.

He drops Cammie off at Shelby's and then drives home. He calls Julian and explains the whole story. "She is bad news," Julian keeps saying. "Change your locks. Block her number. Just forget this ever happened. I *knew* Tess was right. I knew it."

They talk for a half-hour, Gibson not wanting to believe what he knows in his gut is true, not wanting to let Cammie go. "I've never felt this way about anyone, Julian. I've never been this known by anyone."

"I think that's common, with psychopaths. They figure out what you want to hear and they say it," he says.

"No, she's not a psychopath," Gibson says, but he can't deny that she's a thief, and a liar. Eventually he gets in the shower and just lets the hot water envelop him, wondering what he should do about confronting her.

As he is towelling off, he hears a knock on the door. He's terrified it's the cops again, that somehow she has framed him. He pulls on his robe and looks through the peephole, but instead he finds Shelby. Her face is red and streaked with mascara. She's wearing sweatpants and a T-shirt with a stain on the front, and looks so different from the put-together woman he met the night before.

"I need to figure something out," she says. "Can we talk?"

"Sure, come on up." He opens the door wider and backs up to let her in, but she hesitates.

"I'd rather we talk outside."

He realizes then that she is afraid of him.

"Sure, sure. I'll go get dressed, then," he says, expecting her to change her mind and just come in, but she nods. He runs back upstairs, puts on the dirty clothes from the bathroom floor because he can't handle trying to choose a new outfit. He swipes on some deodorant and runs back outside. She is now with her dog, who is sniffing some sidewalk debris. He feels very drawn to Shelby, like they are fighting a similar fight, but he's sure that's a crazy thought. They stand on the sidewalk, and he tries to make himself smaller, less imposing. A few Mormon teenagers from the church down the block jostle around them. They're both afraid to go first.

"Why don't we go to the park? Or a pub, there's one up on Bloor a block over."

"Let's just walk," she says.

Shelby and her dog walk ahead of him south a bit. When she cuts through a parking lot and alley, he walks beside her, knowing they'll end up in Christie Pits, a large park that's like a deep, water-less lake.

"Look, I don't know what Cammie has said about me, but I'm not a dangerous guy. The last thing I stole was a chocolate bar from Woolworths when I was thirteen, and I got stress hives from the guilt. I've never stepped foot in a casino except for a bachelor party one time, and I won five hundred bucks at the slots and then walked away."

"Wow," Shelby says. "But why would she lie to me about that? It's so random."

"I don't know why. I've only been good to her. And in terms of money, I'm usually the one to pay for things. I don't mind it, I offered. But just to be clear, I'm not using her."

"Okay," she says, and points toward a bench that overlooks the park. They sit down awkwardly on either end, with the dog between them.

"It's strange, I've only just met you but I'm inclined to believe you over Cammie, like my gut is telling me to do that," she says. "Which sounds horrible. I don't like feeling this way."

"And I just have to say, my friend Tess, she thinks that Cammie is a liar. Like, a pathological one."

"I've had that thought too, today. Like perhaps it's the only thing that makes sense."

Gibson feels like the floodgates have opened and he can finally express all the things he's been repressing to someone who knows how it feels. He speaks in a near yell, standing up to pace maniacally. "Tess doesn't think she had cancer. And I can't find a record of Morgan ever existing."

"Well, come on. She's had an extremely hard life. I don't think she's evil. Someone lying about cancer is evil. And I met her in grief group. She's definitely lost people close to her—she wouldn't know all that she knows without having experienced it."

Gibson comes back down to earth. He feels cautious again.

"I don't know. None of this adds up. My instincts are screaming at me."

Shelby nods, her brow furrowed. "I have to admit, I feel the same way."

———

Gibson goes to Banjara and gets them some take-out dinner. They find a picnic table and pull out their phones to compare every detail she ever told them about the cancer, about Morgan and her sister. Most of the lies were the same, though she'd told Shelby her dad was dead, but Gibson that he was alive. He's even heard her on the phone with him. Almost everything else was the same, but the timelines were a bit off.

"Why would someone be like this?" Shelby asks. "Like, I'm hardly an example of sanity but this is next level."

"Maybe her sister dying made her go nuts? Grief is a catalyst."

"Maybe—oh my god, maybe!" Shelby can hardly get the words out, and she's banging her fist on the table. It upsets her dog, who starts whining and circling on the ground. Shelby picks him up and gives him kisses. "Sorry, baby, but maybe . . . oh my god, maybe her sister isn't even dead."

"I have to admit, I did consider that," Gibson offers.

They pull up her sister's Facebook feed and both of them ask her to be their friends.

"If she's actually alive, Cammie's a psychopath," he says.

"No, no," Shelby replies. "She's very mentally ill. Who would go to a grief group to mourn a sister who isn't actually dead? And a friend? Unless they were totally nuts."

"Well, the people in the group are pretty vulnerable. Sometimes people target the elderly, people who need others to get by . . ."

Shelby shudders. "That's so bleak. I'd rather imagine she is suffering from some type of intense trauma than purposefully preying on weak people."

"Like, how would we know the difference? I want to confront her. I want everyone to know her lies. Think about how many people she's taken advantage of."

"We need to help her," says Shelby, at the same time that Gibson says, "We need to get even."

"I understand why you're mad. I'm mad too," Shelby says. "But I've given Cammie so much love and care, and she's returned that to me during a very rough time. I don't want to abandon her. She may lie for some deep, traumatized reason, but she's still Cammie. She's still good-hearted."

"Is she? She told me you were a man-hating lesbian who hated me, and that you had a crush on her, and she was only your friend because you let her live there for free and had a lot of money."

"She told me you were a violent gambler and that she was often afraid of you. She implied that bruises on her body were from you. She told me she was broke because you made her give you her money."

Gibson's face drains of colour. "You have to believe me, I would never be violent. I've never touched her in that way, at all. Or any woman. She told me her ex was abusive." It occurs to him now that maybe he misread that interaction with James. "I know I sound defensive, and I know women don't usually lie about that shit. I'm sorry, I just want you to believe me."

They both pack up the take-out containers, and Gibson walks them over to a trash can.

"She said those things because she didn't want us to talk, to figure it out. It was manipulation," Shelby says.

"Yeah, it's so clear now. This is the first time in weeks that the world is making sense again," Gibson says.

"I need to digest this. I appreciate your candour."

She puts her number in his phone.

"Where is she right now? Do you know?" Gibson asks.

"At my place. It's so weird. I don't know what to do."

Shelby's phone buzzes.

"Oh my god," she says, showing him the message: *I can't be alone. I'm afraid I'm going to hurt myself.*

Then Gibson's phone buzzes with a photo of her biting her lip, holding one breast in her hand, with the words *I want you.* He shows it to Shelby, thumb over her nipple.

"I think she's fine. We're both being played. She knows you won't ignore a suicide risk, and she knows I . . . well, she knows what my weaknesses are."

He shakes his head, humiliated.

"I have never felt this stupid and used," he says.

"No, no, you can't let the fact that she played you mean anything about who you are. It's not our fault. Having the instinct to love someone, to be there for them, that's a good thing. Don't lose sight of that."

Gibson doesn't remember the last time he cried in public— perhaps as a child—but he lays his head down on the picnic table and sobs.

12

S helby cries in her car outside Gibson's house. Coach Taylor whimpers and turns circles in the passenger seat. He wriggles onto Shelby's lap, though he knows this isn't allowed, and licks the tears from her face. Shelby laughs. She holds on to Coach tightly and her breath slows. She has never felt so betrayed by someone in her life.

She supposes that she has been lucky. Her parents were consistently present, even if they haven't always been great about her being queer. She's never been cheated on. In fact, when she used to date guys in high school, she often cheated on them just to get out of relationships that bored her so intensely that before she realized she was gay she thought she was missing the part of her brain required to feel attraction. She tries to remember a time when someone lied to her so significantly. The only thing that comes close to this feeling of betrayal is the experience of Kate being gone and having no control over it. The rage she still feels knowing that Kate will never be beside her again, protecting her, loving her. It's unfair to the point of being absurd. She feels a similar anger now at the unfairness of life. That the person who was responsible for shifting the heavy rock of grief in her heart was just a scammer. That she was an easy mark.

It was easy to tell Gibson not to be hard on himself, to honour the parts of him that were open-hearted and trusting. But it is not easy to extend that compassion to herself.

She knows that this is the kind of moment when you should call a friend, not just rely on your dog. But who can she even call to explain what is happening? She can barely remember her other friends. Olive's been travelling all over the United States for a new reality show. When she texts weird photos from small towns, Shelby presses the Haha or Love reaction and doesn't offer anything new. She can't explain it to her mother either.

What can she do, knowing what she knows, and with Cammie asleep in her basement at home?

She decides to drive home, but impulsively pulls over to park on Harbord Street when she sees free tables at a restaurant. She puts Coach in his little portable bed on the chair across from her and orders a cocktail. She's still full from the daal she ate in the park but she doesn't know what else to do. The table next to her is ordering shots and talking loudly about their memories of each other. She tries to imagine having that kind of intimacy and shared narrative with anyone and she can't. She looks at Cammie's last text and tries to think of a way to reply, because what if it is true? What if she's not bluffing?

But she can't imagine just going home and pretending she doesn't know what she knows. What if Cammie is so insane that she becomes violent? What if she tries to hurt her, or Coach? If she thinks so little of Shelby that she'd steal her laptop, her grandmother's jewels, where is the line? Coach knows something is wrong. He looks up at her and whines again. He's as much of a homebody as she is and she's causing him distress.

Then she thinks of the cuts on Cammie's arms and feels some genuine concern that she really will hurt herself. But she knows worry is what Cammie wants her to feel. Cammie wants her to be the mom figure, the sister. She texts back: *Don't do anything stupid. Call Carol Jo or Nancy? I can't come home yet. My mom is in the hospital.* She laughs at how she's now become the liar, but she cannot take care of Cammie right now. She needs to buy herself time.

She pulls out her phone to google "how to tell if someone is a sociopath."

Then she gets a Facebook notification—Cammie's sister has accepted her request. It's one thing to lie about yourself, about your living boyfriend. But to commit fictional murder of your family members for sympathy?

She messages Leslie right away, as bluntly as she feels: *Your sister told me you were dead. I had a feeling you weren't.*

She is unsure that the sister will even reply. I mean, it's a crazy message to get. She sips her cocktail, stares at a woman biking by with a bike basket full of bright fake flowers. She counts to ten and then looks at her messages. Nothing.

A straight couple arrives; you can tell they're in the honeymoon period because their legs are touching under the table and they're staring at each other as though they're the only people on the patio. It's almost embarrassing to watch them because even their stares appear sexual. The woman's face is so open, you can tell she's unconcerned with vulnerability, with this love she's willing to give so openly to someone who could crush it. She twirls her long, wavy blond hair compulsively. The man's bearded face is harder to read, but he's just as enamoured in the moment. Shelby remembers when she and Kate were like that, when even if they were only driving an hour out of town they'd have to stop and have sex in the car on some side road; she'd have bruises on her shins later that she liked to look at. She looks at her phone again; no answer from Cammie's sister, though now she can see that the message has been read.

She finishes her drink and clicks on to HER, the lesbian dating app. She has a profile with a photo of a tree and a fake name, just so she can browse and feel briefly alive sometimes. She scrolls through faces, none appealing.

She finishes her drink, then opens Facebook again. Cammie's sister has written back.

My sister is troubled.

Shelby isn't sure how to respond to that. She wants to prompt Leslie for more but doesn't want to scare her off. She asks the question she most wants to know the answer to: *Did she ever have cancer?*

Our family doesn't think so. She insists that she did. But I believe she probably didn't. I'm relieved to hear from a friend of hers.

Shelby takes this in. She hears her pulse in her ear. She can't believe she has confirmation of the worst lie.

Why would she say you were dead?

Probably because I told her she had to stop lying and pay back the money she stole from me or stay out of my life. She hasn't contacted me since. I worry about her all the time. She talks to our mom. She told Mom you were a big-deal TV executive and she was staying in your Yorkville penthouse and that she was acting now, in a TV show.

I work in the admin office at George Brown. I did get Cammie a job on a TV show, but as an assistant on a reality show.

That sounds more believable.

Was she really kidnapped as a child?

No, I was.

Wow.

He didn't want a kid, though. He drove me around a bit and then dropped me in a park.

Why does she do it?

I don't know. No one else in our family is like this. Our dad is a bit of a liar but that's because he's an alcoholic.

So your dad isn't really dead?

What? No.

She said he killed himself.

He tried to.

Shelby thinks about all the detailed stories Cammie has told in group. How rapt they all were, taking in the goriness of her truth, hugging her and telling her it would all be all right. She pictures Cammie's face and is revolted.

Why does she do it?

I don't know. But she started lying when she was maybe 8, and just never stopped.

What happened when she was 8?

That was when I was kidnapped. And the divorce.

Did she have a friend named Morgan? Who died?

Morgan is real. But she got sick of her shit too. She moved to Niagara Falls.

Wow.

Listen, I'm not sure you'd be into this idea, but I've always imagined that someday we could plan an intervention. Confront her about everything. Get her the help she desperately needs. We're always afraid we're going to get a call, you know, that the worst has happened.

Shelby puts her phone down. She is crying now, pressing her palms against her eyes and trying not to be too obvious about it, but when the server comes over with a sunny "Would you like another, love?" she can't speak, just shakes her head and makes a pen sign with her hand to ask for the bill. The server gives her a pitying look, the kind Shelby has seen so often since Kate died that she doesn't appreciate it anymore.

Shelby's first impulse is to tell Leslie that she'd love to help. That maybe all Cammie needs is to know how much love she has in her life and that she can trust it. Like when people need help with addiction, how friends and family rally around them and give them a chance to clean up. Maybe that's all she needs.

She writes back: *I'd love to help. I'm angry, but I do care about Cammie.*

I'm glad to hear that. Most of her exes or friends end up hating her. She often just changes cities and cons new people. Anyway, I have to get to bed but here's my number. Call anytime and we'll set it up?

———

Shelby pays her bill and walks Coach Taylor around the block until Coach is so tired he just refuses to move. She picks him up and carries him over her shoulder, thinking about how if Cammie is mentally ill, then she can recover. It's not her fault. If it's not her fault, then Shelby isn't the victim of her sadistic manipulations; Cammie is just, as Leslie described, troubled. She feels calmer at this reorientation of the story. She decides she's okay enough to drive home. It's her house. She shouldn't be afraid to go there.

It's quiet when she gets in the door. She turns on all the lights like she used to when she was young and at home alone. She creeps down to the basement. The TV is on, but Cammie appears to be asleep. She thinks about waking her up to confront her but decides against it. She goes back upstairs and wanders around the house, gathering anything she feels is valuable to bring up to her room—paper copies of bills and receipts, the cash she keeps in an envelope by the door for the dog walker or for delivery tips, things that belonged to Kate, like her favourite coffee mug, a framed photo of their wedding. She starts looking for her laptop before she remembers it's already gone. She's just now realizing how much of Kate is on that hard drive. Photos of Kate. Videos. Has Cammie pawned the laptop? She charges back downstairs noisily, hoping Cammie will wake up, but she doesn't. Shelby even turns on the light, but she doesn't stir. She opens up Cammie's knapsack. Her laptop and jewellry aren't in there. She's probably sold everything already.

———————

The calm Shelby felt after talking to Cammie's sister, deciding to help Cammie face her mental illness, is gone. She feels a new surge of rage, stronger than before because the shock has started to subside. She tries to imagine who would win in a physical fight. Probably Cammie, since she is younger and fitter, wiry. Shelby has never fought anyone in her life. She hasn't been exercising at all since Kate died. She goes back upstairs and opens the fridge, and then is overwhelmed with paranoia. If Cammie can lie to her face about everything, would she put drugs in the orange juice? She takes the carton out and pours it down the sink. She finds a carton of sealed peach juice in the cupboard and drinks a glass of that instead. She empties out everything that was already opened in the fridge. She googles "how to tell if something has been poisoned."

Jesus, I'm truly losing my mind.

At the heart of all her concerns is a simple question: Does Cammie really care about her? Does she wish her harm? Was any part of the way Cammie treated her—like a trusted sibling, someone who truly *got* her, someone who would drop anything to listen to her go on about Kate for hours—was any of that real?

Is it just the plain truth that there is no one left alive on earth who would want to listen to Shelby talk about Kate? About the utter despair she's unsure will ever pass? Was she truly an idiot to think Cammie did, that anyone would? She sits down on the kitchen floor, understanding this might be the lowest she has ever been. She didn't think she could arrive at a worse feeling than the grief of those first few months. And yet here she is. All those people saying time would heal, that every thirty days she'd feel a bit better—it was all untrue.

She takes everything into her room, and as she's putting it all in a pile in her closet she wonders, *Did Cammie steal because she's broke? Why didn't she just ask?* Shelby would have given her whatever she needed.

———

She tries to sleep. She just lies awake, cradling Coach, listening for the sound of the basement door opening. She pushes a dresser up against her bedroom door because she feels so unsettled. She wishes she had been brave enough to wake Cammie up and confront her. But she felt scared of how Cammie might react. It is clear she will say anything to anyone to avoid accountability or to get attention or care.

She sends an email to Olive, warning her that Cammie is a liar and a thief and not to hire her again. She apologizes for recommending her, that she didn't know. She doesn't let on how devastated she is, but she says they'll have to have a long breakfast when Olive gets back from her shoot. Then she sends a long email to Carol Jo at three A.M. She tells her everything. Maybe Shelby can confront Cammie in group, and have their support and protection? Shelby is flailing, wanting others to know the truth and to gather near her, help her make sense of it all.

She falls asleep at five A.M., just when she thinks she never will. She's in such a deep sleep that she doesn't hear Cammie getting up and sneaking out quietly. Shelby doesn't wake up until Carol Jo calls her around eight.

Carol Jo doesn't think a confrontation is a good idea. Yes, Cammie's a liar. Yes, a lot of people in the group have figured it out. But it isn't their place.

"Aren't we just indulging her? Enabling her? I feel like no one warned me. You all just watched me get taken for a ride, in my most vulnerable moment. How was that kind, to me?"

"We've all known Cammie a long time. And you have more security than she does. I thought about telling you in the supermarket that day, but I didn't think you'd believe me. People can only change if they want to. And honestly, I do not think Cammie will ever want to. I think she will leave the group and never come back if we confront her. At least now the group gives her some consistency."

"But at what cost?" She feels as angry as Gibson in that moment. Why didn't the people in the group want to take care of *her*?

"I can't believe how toxic that group is. It was my safe space and it turns out everyone was lying to me! Everyone!" Shelby hangs up on Carol Jo. She takes a mason jar out of the cupboard and goes out in the backyard and hurls it against the concrete of the garage.

Not only has Shelby lost the love of her life, but she has lost touch with her closest friends, with a mother who thinks she's indulging herself by grieving and a dad who is great but not at listening to emotions. Shelby has never felt more alone in the world. Cammie was the only person who understood her, and it turns out that wasn't real.

———

She goes downstairs and sees that Cammie has left a dress strewn over the top of the couch, some workout pants on the chair, the sofa bed unmade, the book she was reading, spine split, on the carpet, a dish of her jewellry that she took off before bed and didn't put on again in the morning, a half-eaten power bar. It's obvious she intends to come home and pretend it's all fine and normal. But Cammie doesn't have one of the new keys, so Shelby packs up all her stuff. She notices the tags on her clothes and googles the names—most of them are designer. How did Cammie afford these status symbols? Even the bra Shelby finds in the couch cushions is from Agent Provocateur. The earrings Cammie left on the coffee table are gold and heavy in Shelby's hands. Nothing about Cammie seems cheap. Has she stolen from others?

Shelby stuffs everything into a garbage bag and leaves it on the porch. She texts Cammie that she needs space, it's not working out, your stuff is on the porch. It's passive-aggressive, maybe, but she can't think of any other course of action. She expects Cammie to respond, to ask what's wrong, to offer a listening ear the way she always does. But Shelby gets nothing. Which makes her realize that Cammie must know the jig is up.

It doesn't feel satisfying to know that. She wants to talk to Cammie, clear the air, hear it from her own mouth and try to come to some sort of clarity.

She gets back into bed and takes Kate's hair pomade out of the night table drawer. She inhales deeply and gathers the covers around her.

Olive phones from the car on her way to work, and Shelby unloads some of the craziest details, but she doesn't get the response she expects, especially when she repeats the warning not to rehire her.

"Well, you can't really not hire someone based on this kind of drama," Olive says.

"Drama? She stole my laptop. I'm almost certain she lied about having cancer."

"Well, so she's fucked up. Unless she pulls shit at work it's not like I can tell Andrew to just up and fire her."

"I guess not."

"I'll let him know to keep a close eye but really, I can't do much else."

"It almost sounds like you're on her side."

"No, no. It's just complicated. People like her on the job. She's a riot. Everyone's got problems. No one is completely honest with everyone."

"Wow."

"Look, I'm sorry she's fucking with you, but you just need to establish some boundaries, or sever your friendship and move on."

"I think we're going to do an intervention. Maybe she can get the help she needs?"

"I mean, good luck with that. But I've met scammers before. They just move on down the road to the next mark. She's not going to change. Anyway, I'm at set now, so I have to jet. Let's have breakfast next week?"

"Sure," Shelby says, but she is too pissed to imagine that happening. How can Olive act like this isn't a big deal at all? She hangs up. She was lonely before and is horrified to realize she is now lonelier.

Everything is the same. She's still in the house she never really left. She's still afraid of everything. She pours herself a glass of water and when she drinks it down she realizes that it tastes sweet. She drops the cup and immediately panics. Is the water poisoned? She's really losing it. She remembers finally that her lip gloss is peach-flavoured. She desperately needs some outside perspective.

13

At ten o'clock in the morning Gibson is sitting at his desk, a plastic spoon sticking up in a cup of lime Greek yogurt. He had been hungry. But once the spoon went in he didn't want the yogurt anymore. He sips from a lukewarm glass of water but he knows it's too late. He has that instinctive feeling a migraine is coming on, and once he has that realization it's as though a clock starts ticking. He sticks a Post-it Note on Tina's desk that reads *MIGRAINE! SORRY!* and goes home. He runs two stop signs on a quiet street. He barely makes it there before he throws up violently in the bin outside his apartment door. He crawls up the stairs. His steps are filthy, the woven runner caked with dust and the edges of each white step speckled with dirt. He hasn't had a migraine in a while, but the stress of what is happening with Cammie, and probably not eating or drinking properly, has likely brought it on. Sometimes he goes a full six months without having one and then a high-pressure day will render him housebound. Veda used to know exactly what to do for him when this happened; he'd crawl into bed and she'd bring him cool cloths and close the blackout curtains. She'd make electrolyte drinks and bring him his meds. Shit, he doesn't even have any meds. He texts

Veda the bull's-eye emoji they used to use as shorthand whenever
he had a bad migraine, forgetting this is no longer her concern.
But he likes knowing that someone knows where he is; sometimes
he worries he might die from the pain and nausea, the sensitivity
to even the slightest bit of light. Sometimes they have been so bad
that he's almost wished for it to be so.

He hears the locksmith knocking at five-thirty, when they'd
agreed he'd come by. He can barely text him a *Sorry, can we reschedule*
without the light from his phone stabbing him in the eyes. He goes
in and out of it for hours, and wakes up in the night with a coldness
on his face. It's Cammie, putting a cool cloth on his forehead.

"It's okay, baby, it's okay," she whispers.

"No, no," he mutters, but he isn't sure what he is refusing. He
wants her away from him, from the apartment. He hates being in
a vulnerable state, knowing what he knows about her now, but he
feels powerless to do anything in that moment. He can barely look
at her because he can barely look at anything. She's wearing the red
bra he once told her was seared into his mind forever. He doesn't
so much as fall asleep as fall under the weight of the pain, both the
headache and the grief of losing her.

When he wakes up a few hours later, the pain is lifting and Cammie is asleep beside him. When he sees that the clock reads ten he
isn't sure if it's morning or night until he peels back the blackout
curtains and sees only more darkness. He sits up in bed and drinks
a glass of water, watching Cammie snore, her hands curled up like
a little baby at her neck. Why is she asleep already? He feels the
strange sensation of missing her. Not who she really is, but who he
thought she was. He had such a profound connection with that
person, except none of it was real. Some of it has to have been real.

He goes to the bathroom and texts Shelby, who replies that she is at the bar where Cammie used to work. *I'm very drunk. You know her sister? She's not dead. I talked to her. Come meet me.*

Gibson puts his clothes on and is heading out the door when he turns around. He remembers listening to her stories about her sister's death—elaborate stories of heartache and trauma; he'd held her while she sobbed about it. He feels like his skin is covered in slime. He doesn't want to leave her in the apartment. He wants her gone. He goes back upstairs and wakes Cammie up.

"Your sister is alive," he says.

She sits up, confused.

"No, she's not."

"Yes, she is. I know that, without a doubt."

"Well, my half-sister, Teresa, is alive, yeah. Is that who you mean? We don't speak. Not in years."

He can't stop himself from shouting. "Show me her social media! Show me a photo! Tell me who you mean. You always said you had one sister and she was dead. And that your mom never recovered from her death and blamed you. Why not mention that you had an entire other sister?"

"Because she's a cunt. Come back to bed. I'm not the crazy liar you think I am."

She snuggles back under the covers and closes her eyes. She's like a toddler pretending to be asleep.

He opens Facebook on his phone. He sees that her sister has accepted his friend request. "How can a dead person accept my friend request?"

"It's a fake profile. People impersonate others all the time!"

The way she has an answer for everything makes him want to launch himself into space.

"I know your cancer was fake!"

"Fuck you."

She is up and in his face so quickly he almost stumbles. And then she turns and splits, getting dressed in the hallway. It is too easy for her to be angry, for her to leave.

"Just explain yourself. I will listen if you just tell me the fucking truth for once."

"You're pathetic, you know that? Having cancer was the hardest thing I've ever had to go through. And I did it alone. I'm proud I did it alone. You can't trust anyone in this world to really have your back. I thought I had you. I thought we were a team. I should have known you'd let me down."

Gibson isn't having it. He wants nothing more than for her cancer to be real, but he just *knows*.

"Your cancer was *fake*. You faked it. You fake everything," he says, arms crossed.

She just stares at him. A standstill. Her eyes fill with tears.

"No, you cannot cry. *You* fucked with *me*. *You* played *me*. You are not a victim in this."

"You don't know the real story," she says, sobbing. "You wouldn't treat me this way if you knew the real story."

"So tell me the real story."

"No, I don't trust you. You've shattered the trust that we had."

"Shelby wants to help you, you know."

"You've been talking to Shelby? I knew this would happen. Now it's two against one. Real fair."

"She says you're mentally ill. She wants to help you. But I want to tell everyone about who you really are, a fucking psychopath." He is yelling now, raging at her. She runs down the stairs and out the front door, right into Veda, who is standing in the doorway holding a clear plastic bag with his migraine medication and some broth.

"I thought you might need this, since you sent the text and all. We're still on the same account at the pharmacy."

Gibson starts to cry. "Please, come upstairs."

"Who was that? That girl from the barbecue?"

"It's a long story."

She walks up the stairs, hands him the bag. "Is the worst of it over?"

"Yeah, it was a short one," he says, "but thank you. You're the best. You were always the best."

He watches Veda visibly cringe, as though he'd shone a flashlight in her eyes.

"I'm going to go," she says. "I wasn't ready to see another girl. I mean, I met her that one time but I didn't realize she was still around. I wasn't ready to actually see her here. With you. I want to be your friend, I'm just . . . I don't know. I'm not ready."

"I'm sorry, Veda. I'm sorry. It was so insensitive of me to bring her to Julian's that day."

"It really was."

"Why don't you come in? We could watch a movie?" He is desperate for comfort, to be with someone who really knows him, someone he can trust.

"No, I'm sorry. I can't. I'm glad you're okay, though," she says.

"But I'm not okay," he says pathetically.

"I mean your migraine. You seem fine physically."

She turns to go. Then stops. "She's really like a model. Like, conventionally attractive in a way that is hard to describe."

"I don't know what to say to that. Are you surprised because you think I'm ugly and old now?" He knows as he says this that he's likely never looked worse, never been this pathetic in front of her.

"Of course not. You've always been so handsome to me." She

leans into him, giving him a hug. She smells so familiar. He wants
to kiss her but at least has the sense not to.

"Are you jealous?"

"No. I was just caught off guard. We need boundaries." She
pulls out of the hug. "I shouldn't have come."

"No, no. It was so nice of you to come. I appreciate it."

"I need space still, I'm still too attached."

"Me too! Please, come up. I'm sorry."

She shakes her head. He watches her unlock her bike from a post
and regrets leaving her, regrets ever going home from the bar with
Cammie. He'd prefer a sexless life with Veda over any alternative.

———

He doesn't see Cammie for the next few weeks. It's like she evapo-
rated. Her words *You don't know the real story* haunt him. What if he
was wrong, and he's accused someone with cancer of lying? He goes
to work, he has weekend breakfast with his boys, he plays video
games at Julian's, and he lies awake at night scrolling endlessly
through all of Cammie's social media accounts, looking for clues. In
every photo she posts he looks for a new boyfriend, anticipating that
she will move on quickly, and even with all that he knows, he's
insanely jealous even just thinking about it. In a weak, drunk
moment he texts her, asking if she's okay, and she doesn't respond.

———

He goes over all of it with Shelby, over and over. They meet at the
bar where she used to work, like they are detectives, trying to get
Tommy to talk to them.

"There is something perversely antifeminist about not believing her," Shelby says, taking a first sip of a pale ale. She has been

reading articles and books about why people lie, about antisocial personality disorders, sociopaths. She texts him links with questions like *Borderline? Or narcissist?*

Gibson hasn't been back to the bar since the first few weeks they were dating, when he would sometimes bring her coffee when it was slow. He hasn't lingered inside since the night they met, and he is surprised how different the bar is from how he remembers it in his imagination. Smaller, dingier, a sadder place. It's a busy night and Tommy looks swamped and frustrated, his long blond hair up in a tidy bun. He's wearing a shirt that reads *Hot Nuts.* He takes their orders and they both chicken out of introducing themselves. They are psyching themselves up with a pint first before broaching the topic of Cammie. There are photos of staff on the mirror behind the bar, including several of Cammie posing with a lime rind in her teeth or dancing on the bar. Someone has X'ed out her eyes. Shelby looks like she is barely keeping herself together. She wears an oversized grey one-piece sweatshirt romper and her hair is up in a greasy ponytail.

"Is it weird that when I stop being angry for a few minutes, the feeling that replaces it is longing?" Gibson says. "I miss her."

"No, I totally get it," Shelby says. "All I do lately is research liars, as you've probably realized by my unhinged texts! I've ordered three books from Amazon, spent hours online, reading opinion articles and scholarly research. I listened to a podcast about a woman who got taken in by a con man, and I tell you, he had some of the same behavioural quirks and manipulative tactics that Cammie has. She's like, textbook."

Finally, the next time Tommy comes by, Shelby leans in and says, "Can we ask you some things about Cammie?"

Tommy pauses and squints at them.

"I'm Shelby," she says, and extends her hand for a shake.

"And I'm Gibson," he says, and Tommy gives him a look of recognition. "You were her mark! The last time Cammie and I really had a good time."

"What do you mean, mark?"

"Oh, you know, she'd pick out rich guys and get them to pay for stuff. It was like a game for her. Kind of mean, I thought, but she was a hustler. Like, A-plus grade in the hustle."

"No, no, we dated. I'm not a rich guy. Cammie and I were in a relationship. A real one."

"Okay, well, that's not how it started for her. Sorry to break it to you."

Gibson blushes hard and looks down. He feels ten years old again. Shelby reaches over and squeezes his shoulder.

"We just found out she's a liar. Like, she lied about having cancer, her friends dying, and she stole from me."

Tommy appears unmoved by this revelation. "Yeah, I mean, like I said. Cammie isn't working class, she's criminal class. She looks out for no one but herself. She stole from the till all the time. She used to sell rich kids crushed-up Flintstone vitamins as coke. I'm shocked she's never been to jail, but she can talk her way out of anything. One night I told her my laptop had broken and she convinced a guy to buy her a laptop and had it sent to my place. She worked here for years and no one had the balls to fire her because she'd charm them. But not the new manager—she's been around the block, so Cammie had to go. It's too bad. She was very entertaining. She was a good time and could make us amazing tips, but I never trusted her as far as I could throw her, you know?"

"She said you guys were best friends," Gibson says. "She was devastated when you didn't want to be her friend anymore."

"I told her to give the money back. She wouldn't admit she was the thief. It was bananas. But yeah, we weren't best friends. We partied a lot. We got sloppy. I guess we were close in that way, sometimes."

He leaves their table and Shelby says, "Wow, I nursed her through an epic night where she sobbed about losing Tommy, saying that he was the closest person to her."

"That's really sad," Gibson says. "I mean, not as sad as me thinking that someone who looked like her would pick me up in a bar, I guess."

"No, no. Remember, that could have been a lie she told Tommy. We can never know what was true or not. And she's not someone who sticks around people she doesn't like; she obviously liked being around you."

"I feel truly pathetic," Gibson says, taking gulps of beer.

"I know. I do too. But we're not. We have good hearts. We shouldn't be mad at ourselves for assuming the best about someone. You know, in all the articles the experts say that liars pick people who seem sensitive and empathetic, because we're easier to manipulate. I'm not going to be ashamed of being sensitive and caring about people."

"I guess," Gibson concedes. "I can think that and it's comforting, but I don't feel it."

Shelby scrolls on her phone and then reads a line from an article. "'Just as trust is a default of human interaction, a presumption of sincerity is a default expectation of basic communication.' A social scientist who is an expert on persuasion said this. See? Most people trust on instinct. It's human nature."

"You're not going to let me feel like a chump, are you?"

"Not on my watch!" She smiles warmly at Gibson, and despite her raggedy appearance he starts to feel a bit of an attraction to her.

"I'm glad we're friends. You're making me feel sane these days," she says.

He gets up to go to the bathroom and every inch of the bar reminds him of the night of Julian's party. How Cammie looked bent over the pool table, where they kissed by the jukebox after she selected the song "November Rain" and made a persuasive case for it being Guns N' Roses canon. How she sat on his lap in the corner booth after bringing him shots of tequila and whispered, *I think the universe wanted us to meet.* All these moments that felt fated and magical and are now tawdry and cornball.

When he gets back to Shelby she's got her phone open to Cammie's Instagram. She's just posted a photo of a new tattoo of a collie dog on her arm. The caption reads: *Nina.*

"Nina is a statue of a dog she found one night, the first night we hung out. This is so bananas," she says.

"She told me Nina was a collie she had growing up who died in a barn fire." He's not sure why but this makes him laugh.

"Do you watch her stories?"

"I don't want her to see that I've seen them."

"I still click sometimes, but I guess it's less loaded for me," Shelby says, clicking on a new story. It's a photo of Cammie with the tattoo artist, a girl with blunt baby bangs and cheek piercings. The text reads *My new bestie!!*

"They move on quick to new people," Shelby says. "I guess that's true. That's a bit sad, isn't it? Like, ultimately she is a very sad, desperate person. And I feel very lonely these days, but she is truly alone. If you can't connect with anyone authentically, as yourself, that is almost worse than death, is it not?"

"I don't know. She seems to be having a fucking good time at life," he says. He clicks on the next story and it's her and the tattoo girl drinking on a patio, with the words *Fuck All Men.* He's morose. He knows he should go home. He's starting to feel angry again, and he'd hoped that Shelby's intellectual curiosity about Cammie's pathology, and her empathy, would soften the rage and betrayal he can't seem to get away from.

"I feel like we need to help her. At least let her know that we're here and we can be a resource, you know? What if she can change?"

"Have you known a lot of people to change?"

"Yes. Kate changed. She used to be addicted to speed in college. She did all sorts of things she regretted. Then she got sober and became the most steady, empathetic person I've ever met in my life. Can someone become addicted to lying? I guess it's just about whether or not she's a true sociopath or if she, I don't know, has some other diagnosis, like undiagnosed PTSD, which would mean she can change."

"Do you remember what she's like when confronted? She doesn't take even one bit of responsibility. She turns it around on whoever accuses her, no matter how gently. I don't think that is the behaviour of someone who is capable of self-awareness, someone who doesn't want to hurt people. She's fucked. She's just fucked!"

Shelby reaches over and grabs his hand. "Your anger is a normal reaction and it's okay. I'm angry too. I just feel better when I think of this whole situation as an opportunity to help her transform her life. You know? Like maybe this happened for a reason, so she has us, these two people who love her, and maybe that means she can finally let go of these behaviours that no longer serve her?"

"Tommy said she called me her *mark*. Have you seen the movie *Catch Me If You Can*? There are people who pretend to be surgeons!"

"Yeah, my research says women pretend to be sick and men pretend to be doctors. Isn't that fucked?"

"So fucked."

"But, Gibson, what if we can help? Shouldn't we at least try? We're obviously both still so affected."

"I'm obsessed. It's all I think about," Gibson admits.

"I think we should call her sister and say yes to the intervention idea."

"Okay," he says. "Okay. I may as well try to do good instead of just being mad forever."

Shelby takes out a notebook. "Let's make a list of people in her life, and choose a day and a place and make it happen."

———

Gibson is very drunk when he gets home, the kind of intoxicated where he eats pizza in bed without a plate or a care in the world. Right before dawn his phone buzzes over and over, and he wakes up to six missed calls, then his doorbell and a text from Cammie. She's downstairs.

He calls to her out the window. She flashes him in response. *Oh man. I shouldn't go to the door,* he says, but he rinses his mouth and rubs at his face, in a dizzy and dehydrated dream. *Don't answer the door, you fucking lunatic,* he mutters as he walks down the stairs toward the door. He rests his forehead against the tempered glass. He can see a blurry Cammie shape behind it. He hears her singing *Come on, Gibson* to the tune of "Come On, Eileen." She's drunk too. He opens the door a crack and she shoves her arm through, gripping the door frame.

"It's your worst nightmare," she says in a weird devilish voice, and pushes her way inside and slams the door dramatically.

"We are meant for each other!" she yells. "You and I, you know this. You know we are."

"Shh, my neighbours," he says, but she pushes him down on the bottom stair and kisses him. It's sloppy and weird and he's not sure what to do. She tastes like whiskey and mint gum. Her hands smell like chicken wings. They half crawl upstairs, pawing at each other, and she mumbles, "I need you, I need you." He fucks her against the banister in the hall. She keeps pleading, "Harder," but he goes at the pace he wants, even though he feels so much rage. She says, "Hurt me, bite me," and he doesn't. He's not being nice, he just doesn't get off on hurting women and he wants to get off. He wants to feel this good with her one last time. After he comes he feels the same way he does when the porn is still playing on his laptop and it looks vile and he feels weird. He gets her a glass of water while she pees, the way he usually does. He watches her drink it. He always used to make her come first, but this time the sex is over and they both know it. He picks up her dress from the hallway floor and says, "I need some space. Do you mind going?" He says it with a gentleness in his voice because he is afraid of her.

She makes a huffing sound, crosses her arms.

"You're a fucking asshole," she says, gathering her bag.

"So are you," he says.

She gives him a weird smirk, and he knows what the smirk means: she could destroy him if she wanted to.

"Please," he says. "I just need to sleep. By myself."

He expects to have a big fight about this, but she doesn't resist. She just does the final button up on her dress and walks down the stairs, and he watches from the window as she crosses the street and lies down on her back on a bench at the bus stop, her knees up, one arm over her eyes, the other arm putting her flat purse under her shirt to keep from getting robbed. She looks like she's done this a million times.

He knows then that all the times he's protected her, saved her, bought things for her, it was theatre. She never needed him, even once, to save her from anything.

14

As the days grow shorter and red leaves glut the gutters on streets in the Annex, the calendar on Shelby's fridge is bare except for one square that reads *INTERVENTION* in blue for two weeks from now.

She eats five orange Tic Tacs and a handful of stale salt-and-vinegar chips for breakfast, pulls on a pinkish-grey romper made of sweatshirt material to walk Coach to the coffee shop on Harbord. It has a hood, so she pulls it close around her face, a warm hug for the greasy hair she doesn't want to do anything about. She avoids her reflection in shop windows, staring down at Coach's chubby wrinkled body as he bunnies along. She blows the foam heart on her latte and takes a sip that allows for the first feeling of real pleasure she's had since yesterday's coffee. She sits on the bench outside the café, feeling pleasantly invisible watching the pretty hipsters linger with their dogs and coffees. She is aware that it's the day of grief group and she is not going. The handful of hours between now and the group's starting time will be heavy and loud, but as soon as the group is over she'll get the lightness she craves, the freedom of answering to no one, of not being witnessed.

She pockets her phone and walks back home. Coach immediately hops up on the couch because he's so used to them spending the day on it like it's a raft at sea. She puts her phone down and pours herself a glass of water. She takes two ice cubes out of the tray, and instead of putting them in the glass, she presses them against her chest. It's supposed to stimulate the vagus nerve, she's been told. It doesn't help. She puts them on her eyes next. They are tired from the eighteen tabs she has open on her new laptop with articles about liars, antisocial personality disorders, Munchausen's, con artists. She tries to do other things but she keeps going back to the personal essays and *DSM* diagnoses and clinical texts, trying to find out why Cammie is the way she is. When she shuts her laptop, she often opens the books she's ordered on PTSD and pathological lying, borderline personality disorder, sociopathy in women. She digs out her old highlighters from the junk drawer and highlights sentences, thinking she's finally figured it out, and then something else pops up in another possible diagnosis and she thinks she understands what Cammie's pathology might be.

While reading about narcissism she starts to go a bit loopy—maybe she herself is narcissistic? She does spend a lot of time worrying, mostly about her own death, her own safety. What's that if not self-involved? She starts to remember when her OCD was particularly bad and she became obsessed with being a good person. *Would a good person make this choice?* she asked herself nearly constantly. As she looks at every aspect of Cammie's character, she starts to think about her own. Is she always honest? When does she lie? People lie all the time and don't realize they're doing it. She opens the Notes function in her phone and decides to make a list of all the lies she tells in a day.

She runs her fingers through her hair and gets stuck in the greasy knot of curls and knows she has to shower, as torturous as taking off her clothes and turning on the taps feels. When she finally does it she douses herself in two-in-one shampoo, a cheap brand she'd never buy, but she remains at the mercy of whatever her mother brings over because the last time she was in the drug-store the lights and sounds made her physically ill. While shaving under her arms she thinks she feels a lump and starts to panic. She's not sure when she became obsessed with swollen glands, but any sign of them can cause her an all-consuming type of anxiety. She gets out of the shower, dripping suds onto the dusty-pink bath mat, and wipes a palm across the steam before examining herself in the bathroom mirror. The right armpit looks different from the left, but did it always? It occurs to her in this moment that her health anxiety feels like it is not up to her; she cannot control it. She's tried nearly every form of therapy and it persists. What if this is what Munchausen's feels like? What if Cammie is absolutely convinced that she did have cancer, having hallucinated or lived through a delusion in a more material way that made her imagine chemotherapy was real? What if she loses time, dissociates, believes every word out of her own mouth? At least Shelby knows on some level when she is being crazy. What if Cammie doesn't? She gets back in the shower and stands under a stream of too-hot water, appreciating the burning feeling on her neck and shoulders. It is a strange state of mind to be both somewhat suicidal and afraid of swollen glands; should a suicidal person welcome an illness to take them out? But no. It's about control. Isn't everything?

The more she reads about PTSD and pathological lying, the more Cammie's rehabilitation becomes Shelby's main goal. Every time her phone buzzes she expects it will be Cammie, and she dreads it but is also disappointed when it isn't her. She has read so many articles about why people lie, what traumas can inspire women to create these alternate life stories, that she begins to feel sympathetic and determined to help Cammie change her life.

Even if Cammie was driven to behave in ways that push people away, the friendship they had was real. Cammie did help Shelby out of her slump of unmovable grief. And Shelby believes she helped Cammie materially and provided her with a familial comfort she lacked, a consistent place to be herself.

After all, Shelby doesn't think she'd still be here if people in her life hadn't supported her through the worst of her OCD and anxiety disorder. Before she met Kate, Olive used to walk with her to the grocery store during the worst months of her agoraphobic period, back when she was so afraid to have a panic attack that she could barely leave her house. Kate helped her through a bad winter depression and lots of panic attacks. They didn't leave her in a crisis. Maybe it's time for Shelby to pay that karma back and help Cammie, even though her mental health issue impacts others in a significantly different way.

She studies for the intervention as though it is a school project she is going to be graded on. She gets through that first night without grief group, and then the next week. She slips back into her old routines. She calls in sick to work again for a few too many days in a row, and then her boss calls and says she might want to apply for long-term disability. Instead of that waking her up and pushing her back to work, as her boss intends, she just mumbles yes, that's a good idea. She doesn't need to apply for it, though, because she has Kate's life insurance. It feels weird and morbid to use this giant sum of money from Kate's death for her life. But she is getting close to having to use it. The one time she accessed it she spent six hours donating to GoFundMe accounts, mostly for bail funds and hospital bills for queer and trans people in the United States without health insurance, some queer kids who needed rent and bills paid for, things Kate would have donated to anytime she came across someone asking.

She decides to walk by the door to the JCC near the time the group begins. She picks up a bouquet of flowers at the shop on Harbord on the way, something that a grief book suggested she do for self-care. She leans against a cement planter filled with dead plants and cigarette butts across the street and watches for Cammie to arrive. When it's five minutes past the group start time and Cammie still hasn't arrived, she decides to go in. She feels more nervous than the first time, but if Cammie isn't there, why shouldn't she go? She can even talk about the devastating impact Cammie's behaviour has had on her mental health. She has just as much of a right to be there as anyone else, after all. She'll ice Carol Jo, sure. But everyone else likely has no idea. And instead of focusing on Cammie she should focus on her own healing. Maybe talk more in group, use it as more of a resource. Maybe Cammie was a distraction, not a help.

In the elevator up to the group she practises things she might say to Cammie:

I know you have problems, we all have problems. But what if the people who love you supported you on a journey to tell the truth?

Cammie, I love you but you hurt me and you hurt Gibson, and I think you have serious mental health issues that you're not addressing, and I'd like to help you, if you'll let me.

Carol Jo raises her eyebrows when Shelby walks in, but she smiles warmly. Her smile used to brighten Shelby's day, but now it makes her suspicious. It's a performance smile. After all, she cares more for Cammie's well-being than Shelby's. Shelby glares at Carol Jo and sits as far as possible from her chair, leaving her now-wilting bouquet in a lump beside her purse at her feet. What is she doing here?

While the first people share, Shelby's brain is elsewhere. Why has she come? What should she say? She is conscious of every bodily sensation. She notices a scratch on her arm she hasn't seen before, and a series of small bruises. How many bruises are too many? It's a sign of leukemia, after all. Her nails are brittle. Low iron again?

Just as she is debating taking out her phone and googling "first signs of leukemia," the door opens and in walks Cammie. Smiling brightly, like she hasn't a care in the world.

Shelby's whole body is instantly on alert with rage. Every patient thing she imagined saying to her evaporates. Cammie volunteers to share immediately after the woman who was initially talking ends her share.

"Well, my half-sister, Teresa, got back in touch, though I swore I'd never talk to her again after how she acted at my sister's funeral."

Shelby scoffs. She'd asked Cammie's real and alive sister who Teresa is, and apparently she is a stepsister who lived with them for six months in high school when their mother briefly remarried.

Shelby finds Cammie's performance in the group almost terrifying. She watches her speak and realizes that she has no idea what Cammie's limits are. Who knows how far she would go to preserve this fake identity. She feels like she might throw up, so instead she stands up and starts toward the door. As she walks she tries to breathe steadily and picture being home, with Coach Taylor, in her grounded place.

"Was it something I said?" Cammie's voice hits her in the back like an arrow.

"Cammie, don't," she hears Carol Jo admonish her.

Shelby turns to the group, holding the door frame for support.

"Cammie's sister is alive. She's lying. She has a mental illness. Nothing she says here is true."

Cammie looks stunned at first, like a deer in headlights, and then launches into her charade.

"That's not true at all. Shelby is just trying to get back at me. You know, cancel me, pretend I'm the crazy one."

"None of you warned me about her, even though you all know the truth. Carol Jo knows you're a liar, she told me you're a liar, and she just lets you take advantage of everyone you meet."

"Shelby, I didn't say she was a liar. I don't name-call like that," Carol Jo starts to say.

"Yes, you *did,* oh my god! This whole group is toxic! I can't believe I used to look forward to coming here." Shelby bolts, for fear of losing her mind in the depth of denial in the room.

Nancy follows her out to the elevators, where Shelby sobs and presses at the already-orange down button. Nancy twists the grey braid she always wears to one side as she speaks.

"You know, I was going to tell you, so many times. I was going to warn you. But I just didn't know what was right."

"Nobody cared enough to warn me! Carol Jo implied that I'm the stronger one, and I'm barely functioning, Nancy."

"I know. I know. I'm sorry," she says, twisting her braid again. She looks like a helpless little kid, not an adult with more life experience than Shelby.

"This group should have a therapist, you know, or some rules."

"Well, it's supposed to be peer to peer. That's the philosophy." Maybe Nancy isn't helpless and passive; maybe she thinks she's right.

"It's a dangerous philosophy!"

"Maybe," Nancy says, "but honestly, what's better, to turn Cammie away?"

"Yes. She needs people to call her on her bullshit. She's a vampire. Pretending she isn't using people is failing her just as much."

"You know, everyone has a complicated relationship with the truth. Especially addicts, people who have addicts in their families. It's not as simple as you're making it out to be. I don't want to expel Cammie from the only consistent community she has."

"Cammie is not a child." Shelby crosses her arms, and so does Nancy. They face each other like two characters in *The Lorax* by Dr. Seuss.

"No, she's not. But sometimes I think she's arrested at a certain age. Sometimes that happens with trauma."

"Great, so am I going to emotionally arrest at thirty-two because of this trauma, then?"

"What should we do with people who don't seem to understand the truth? Cast them aside? Imprison them?"

"I don't have the answer to that, but if someone was standing in traffic all day long, you'd take them out of traffic. If someone was throwing rocks at puppies, you'd make sure they stopped. Just because Cammie's crimes are emotional torture and not physical torture doesn't mean they are less violent."

"Well, I think there *is* a distinction between lying and actual violence," Nancy says.

"Jesus Christ, why did you even follow me out here? Why don't you just go back in there and continue feeding baby Cammie her bottle? She is not going to learn *anything* from this."

"I wanted to make sure you were okay."

"No, I'm not okay. And no, you didn't. You wanted to cover your own ass. I'm not okay at all. I am worse than I was when I first arrived at this group. Because I lost my wife. And now I've lost the only support I had for having lost my wife, and my attitude about life and my faith in humanity is fucking shattered!" Shelby is screaming now, and a security guard approaches. She holds up her hands. She sees Cammie poke her head out of the doorway and smirk at her. Shelby feels for the first time in her life capable of harming another human being. Instead she turns toward the *EXIT* sign on the stairwell door and runs down three flights, and then out onto the street and all the way home.

Shelby is never going to return to the group again.

She calls Gibson. "Fuck the intervention," she says. "I'm not hosting it."

"We can do it at my house," he says. "Just come. Please. I can't do it without you."

When is anyone going to actually take care of *her*?

That is all she wants. When she had a bad day at work or with anxiety, Kate used to pour her a bath with Epsom salts and rose petals and wash her hair and then tuck her in with the weighted blanket and let her watch the dating reality show that Kate loathed with every fibre of her being. She'll never have that again.

Shelby gets in her car and drives north. Once she gets to Allen Road, she drives just as fast and crazy as most people do, and for the first time she doesn't feel scared. She's reckless in a way that she knows means she shouldn't actually be driving, but she doesn't care. She ends up at the cemetery where Kate is buried in her family plot. She parks next to a sign that says *No Parking*, and she doesn't care. She is ready to fight anyone who says she can't be here. She gets the camping chair out of the trunk, and the wool blanket she keeps in the back seat for emergencies, and she sits beside Kate's grave like she did the first week after the burial. Fuck everyone else.

She is stuck in a kind of lucid nightmare, where she can't go back and can't seem to figure out how to go forward. "It turns out you're the only reason I liked being here," she mumbles to Kate's headstone. "On Earth, I mean."

It's not fair.

She's waiting for some kind of divine intervention, some whisper from the heavens that all is going to be well. She'll even accept a bird or a rainbow or a terrible sudden wind, a weird stranger yelling something prophetic at her. But the graveyard is quiet. The dead are being obedient and calm. She crushes red leaves in her palm. She wipes her nose on her sleeve. She is starting to feel sleepy when her phone rings. It's a weird number, and she answers "Yeah?" because she no longer cares about being nice to anyone at all.

"Shelby Roberston?"

"Yes."

"I'm calling from Alpine Credit. You're listed as a guarantor for a personal loan to Camilla Parker. She hasn't been making her minimum payments and I'm calling you to inquire about when we might expect the payments to resume."

"I did not sign anything. Ever. I don't even know Camilla Parker . . . anymore."

"We have your signature on file, and your contact information. If you'd like to dispute this there is a formal process and—"

Shelby just hangs up and blocks the number.

In the next week three more creditors call asking for Cammie. One tells her, "You're listed as a co-signer on a line of credit."

"That can't be possible. . . . I never signed anything," she says. She calls her mom, asks if she knows a lawyer.

She also starts getting text messages from unknown numbers.

You're Going to Regret What You Did.

You think you're so kind, but you're really a hypocrite.

She answers them all the same way: *Cammie, I know it's you. I'll only talk to you if you want to change. I'm open to helping you.*

Cammie never responds.

15

Gibson cleans his apartment, unpacking the final box, which contains an old camera, a Lego-frame photo of his parents, pencil crayons from high school he can't seem to throw away, a stack of old birthday cards from his grandmother, and three books in the business self-help genre he'd be embarrassed to put on his shelf. Who was he when he packed his old house up and left, alone for the first time since college, unravelling in a one-bedroom on the second floor of a crumbling Victorian on Ossington Avenue? Those first few weeks were a blur of self-loathing and sadness, and then Cammie arrived to make him come alive again. They painted and unpacked his place, and in a way it became their place. But this one box sat stubbornly under the kitchen table, still taped up, and he never got to it until now, suddenly aware that he cares very much what Cammie's sister thinks of his apartment, despite her being a stranger.

He sets out snacks—a trio of cheeses on a kidney-shaped plate with tiny copper knives, a bowl of rye crackers, a fistful of dried apricots, pickled green beans, and a cheerful tiny bowl of cherry tomatoes. He redusts every surface and drinks another cup of coffee, wondering what he hopes to achieve by intervening so formally in Cammie's mental health crisis. Is it a crisis if she's been this way for her entire adult life?

He is pacing the back patio when he hears the doorbell. He checks his hair in the small mirror Cammie tacked up by the door. She used to do her lipstick in it before leaving. Cammie's sister looks so much like a slightly older, more conservative version of Cammie that he finds it difficult to look her in the eye. She hands him a bottle of Perrier and a box of custard tarts from the nearby Portuguese bakery.

"Hi, I'm Leslie. Nice to meet you," she says. "God, this is awkward, isn't it?"

"It sure is," he laughs, "but I'm grateful you're here."

They walk upstairs. The tarts shake back and forth in the box as he ascends the steps, and he looks around at his apartment as though taking it in from her perspective. It looks like a sad single dad lives here. Except he doesn't even have a kid. He feels pathetic for falling in love with a younger woman, for this life he thought he wanted. Then he looks at Leslie, looking for signs of instability, signs that the trauma of their upbringing also had an impact on her psyche somehow. He desperately wants signs that Cammie is the way she is through no fault of her own, and that she can heal, live a better life, the way her sister appears to.

"It's her birthday today," Leslie says. He opens the box of tarts and arranges them on a plate. They're bright yellow, with bursts of oval caramel burns on top. He offers them to her. She takes one.

"Really? She didn't tell me!"

"She always has a bit of a pity party on her birthdays. My mother was going to come, but she cancelled last minute. Said she didn't think it would work, that she didn't want to drive all the way here for nothing. I thought doing it on Cammie's birthday would make her come for sure, but that's my mom for you," she says, taking a bite of the tart. "Jesus Christ, these are good. I miss living around here. I used to buy these in university."

Gibson immediately feels judgmental of their mother, like obviously Cammie's parents fucked her up in some way and now her mother isn't even trying to take responsibility for it.

"Coffee?" he offers, and she nods. The coffeepot is full; he remade it twice so it would be fresh when she arrived. He pours it into a mug with Burt Reynolds's face on it that Cammie brought home from Value Village. "Did a lot fall on you growing up?" he asks, and then feels bad for asking, as he places a small blue carton of half-and-half and the sugar bowl in front of her on the table.

"Indeed. A common thing in my Al-Anon group, quite frankly."

He isn't sure what to say to that. He really wants to have a beer, but given what she's just said, he decides instead to have another coffee despite already feeling anxious from the two previous cups. He puts a spoonful of sugar in it, though he usually takes it unsweetened, just so it feels like a different drink.

"So, she should be here in about half an hour. She thinks she's just coming to collect her things." He points toward a duffel bag and a box filled with toiletries, a shirt, her gym shoes. "I don't know if Shelby will actually come. She's very angry. She's been flip-flopping between wanting to help Cammie and wanting to just end their friendship entirely."

"I understand that," Leslie says. "Cammie's life has been a series of short, very intense friendships with people who eventually never speak to her again."

"The weird thing is, I still love her, in so many ways."

"Well, that's Cammie for you. I've been watching men walk over glass shards for her for her entire life. I don't know why she inspires such loyalty."

Gibson feels some shame at that, takes a too-large sip of coffee, and coughs. He doesn't want to talk about sex with Cammie's sister. He feels weak again.

"I'm sorry, I don't mean to imply your relationship wasn't genuine," Leslie says.

"Do you know where she's been lately?"

"I assumed she found some other guy to hang out with, frankly, but my mom told me she went back to staying with our dad."

"Did you know that she told Shelby he'd killed himself?"

"He tried," she says dryly. If Cammie is the dramatic charmer, Leslie is her complete opposite. Straightforward, sharp, kind but firm.

"Oh."

"But I know she's in the city today because apparently she's got another job with a reality TV show, so she's looking at apartments."

"Wow, she's just going to keep on keeping on, like nothing major happened?"

"That's her MO, generally. She always finds someone to take care of her. I've spent a lot of time worrying about getting a call from a psych ward or a homeless shelter but she never quite lands there. It's almost impressive."

———

Shelby arrives next, with her dog, looking shakier than Gibson has ever seen her. Shelby unpacks a folding playpen and puts Coach Taylor in it, giving him some treats and a belly rub. She is wearing an assemblage of clothes from Mountain Equipment Co-op, and her hair is up in a ponytail, but she looks like she hasn't slept in weeks. She shakes Leslie's hand awkwardly and accepts a coffee, takes one sip, and her hand shakes so much she has to put the mug down so she doesn't spill. She takes a tart and eats it in two giant bites. Gibson is happy to see her; he feels like they survived a shipwreck together and if he weren't afraid of being weird he'd be calling her all the time. Her presence makes him feel less crazy.

"I'm so glad you're here. I think about texting you all the time, but I don't want to bug you," he says, taking another sip of coffee.

"You can always text me. That's so nice. I'm really shaky right now because someone threw a rock through my window earlier," she says. "My dad is over there now fixing it. I'm afraid to go back there. Do you think she would do something like that?"

Leslie looks shocked. "Honestly, she's never been violent. She accuses other people of violence, or she's violent to herself, but never to others."

"She signed my name as a co-signer for a bank loan. Creditors won't stop calling me. I called the police and filed a report on her."

"Well, *that* is classic Cammie. I hope you never shared passwords with her."

"I did. I gave her my debit card a bunch of times to buy groceries," Shelby admits. "I'm such a sucker!"

"You should probably change your SIN number, keep a record of everything in writing, and get a lawyer." Leslie says it in such a deadpan way, like these kinds of revelations about her sister are mundane and commonplace. "She bankrupted our aunt Cheryl."

Shelby paces, wandering into the bedroom at the front of the apartment. Gibson follows her, feeling weird that she's in his bedroom, but none of the rooms have doors, so it makes sense she'd wander and assume it was a living room. She stands at the window overlooking the street.

"You all right? Sorry, my bedroom is a bit of a mess," he says, even though he'd spent the morning cleaning.

"Oh my god, she's outside, with Carol Jo, a lady from our grief support group."

She says it loud enough that Leslie hears from the kitchen and comes to the window. They watch her and Carol Jo sitting on the bench. Cammie is talking emphatically, using her hands.

"Literally no one has ever died in our family. We live for-fucking-ever with our pickled organs. Dad has one leg now and he's never gonna die. Who could she be grieving?"

"You, I guess, in her imagination," Gibson says.

"She told me her dad was dead," Shelby says. "Which is weird because she was otherwise so careful to tell us the exact same lies."

The doorbell rings. They all look at each other as if to say, *Oh shit, now we really have to do this.* Gibson wishes he could exit his skin, just be a skeleton running out to jump over the back patio. But he keeps his promises, and he does want to follow through. He tells himself that later that night he can have a beer and forget about this awful day. He walks down the staircase to the front entry and opens the door. Cammie is wearing a long cardigan over the red romper she wore the night they met. It isn't sexy anymore, it's kind of child-like. But when Gibson catches her eye, he loses his footing. Why is he so attracted to her, why even now would he love nothing more than to kiss her, even though she hurt him so much? He's suddenly concerned he'll never have sex like that again, animalistic, so passionate it made previous sexual experiences feel like handshakes.

Carol Jo glares at him.

"I'm Gibson." He reaches out to shake her hand but she doesn't offer it back.

"Come on up," he says, afraid and uncertain about what Cammie will do when she sees everyone in the kitchen. They follow him. Carol Jo takes each stair slowly, so he's standing at the top with Leslie and Shelby sitting at the kitchen table as her head slowly crests the top.

"We're just here to get Cammie's things," Carol Jo says, in an oddly formal way, as she hovers at the top, leaning on the banister. Leslie stands up from the table and approaches her.

"I'm Leslie, Cammie's sister," she says. "Hey, Cammie, happy birthday."

Cammie looks shocked, and Gibson realizes that it's authentic shock. He can see the difference now. She stays on the staircase, gripping one of the wooden posts of the banister, behind Carol Jo.

"Why don't you both come sit down, have some tea or coffee?" Leslie says, motioning farther into the kitchen.

Carol Jo glares at Gibson.

"Gibson isn't abusive, Carol Jo. Whatever she's told you isn't true," Shelby says.

Carol Jo looks conflicted at this information.

"Well, she's asked me to be here with her."

So far this isn't going the way they planned. Maybe they should have included Carol Jo in the planning. They didn't anticipate that Cammie would arrive with a protector.

"Why don't you come sit down, Cammie," says Shelby, pointing to the chair they'd hoped she'd sit in.

"No," says Cammie, and she crosses her arms. "What's going on? I feel like I'm being ambushed."

"This is an intervention about the lying. If you would like some help, we are here to offer it," Leslie says.

"You fucking bitch," Cammie says. "You're such a traitor."

Leslie winces, and Shelby takes over. "We love you, and we want you to get help to be your real self."

Cammie scoffs.

"We know you never had cancer. That Morgan is alive. That obviously your sister is alive," Shelby says.

"Yeah," Gibson says, weakly.

"Are you open to hearing our ideas?" Leslie says. "We're here because we love you and care about you and want you to get well."

Cammie looks like a caged animal, her eyes bugging out of her head. She knows she cannot charm her way out of this. She is caught.

"Cammie, do you want to sit and talk? It might be good to hear them out," Carol Jo says gently.

"*I did too* have cancer. That you are all ganging up against me right now, after all I've gone through, it's disgusting. You're disgusting people."

"Cammie, you don't need to name-call," says Carol Jo, like a nursery school teacher.

For a moment they are all silent. Leslie finally stands up again, filled with a sibling type of rage.

"No one in your life, literally no one, has ever seen any evidence that you were ever sick. You made it up in a moment of desperation and now you can't get out of it. Don't you want to feel free from it, from the lying? You've been doing it since you were a little kid. Everyone knows. There's a reason why you can only keep scamming new people. But we're still here. We still love you."

"You're the liar right now, Leslie."

"I called Princess Margaret on one of the days you were supposedly having radiation treatment. No one had ever heard of you," Leslie said.

"And you know that I called the ERs. You admitted to lying! Wouldn't it feel good to just let it all go?" Gibson pleads.

"And you may not have cancer but you are sick," Shelby says, "just mentally. Don't you want to get well?"

Cammie has a look on her face that reminds Gibson of a raccoon he once cornered in a garage. He can see it in her eyes, the capability of violence. She's never going to let the delusion go. He knows it now.

"You're all abusive, after all I've done for *all* of you. I practically raised you, Leslie! And I get no support. I went through chemo by myself. You're all so selfish, and delusional. Do you know what it was like to get treatment beside people who always had family with them? The looks of pity I'd get? *You're the liars. I want nothing to do with you ever again.*"

She grabs her duffel bag and box of things and runs down the stairs and out the door.

Carol Jo looks at them helplessly. "You tried your best, guys. I don't think she's ready to face reality. She has to decide that for herself, when she's hit rock bottom. You're really Leslie, her sister, a paramedic?"

"Yes, I was a paramedic, yes. Now I'm a housewife."

"I can't believe it. I thought that out of every story she told, the one about you, the one that brought her to the grief group, would be true. I thought your death was the reason she told stories."

Carol Jo shakes her head back and forth. She suddenly looks incredibly old.

" 'Telling stories' is a real euphemism," Leslie says.

Carol Jo nods again, then leaves.

It's over. They look at each other like their team just lost a game. Leslie gathers her things and runs after Cammie. Gibson and Shelby watch from the window as Leslie watches Carol Jo and Cammie drive away. She waves up at them and gets in her SUV. They never see her again.

———

By eight he's back looking at Cammie's Instagram. She's with the tattoo girl again. They're at a shooting range. The caption reads: *Happy 30th to me!* She posts a photo where she's in a very short skirt, holding a rifle. He jerks off to it and afterward feels like dying.

He gets a text from Shelby an hour later. She's hiding in her closet.

He drives to her house, drumming on the steering wheel, swerving around the corner from Ossington to Harbord, running a stop sign. If he didn't have to sit still to drive he would be running; it feels like he has been shot out of a cannon. He thinks about the look on Cammie's face at the end of the intervention, how capable he thinks she is of violence, how she's just posted photos of herself with a gun. Visions of poor Shelby, already such a fragile woman, hiding in her closet just make him livid. A very slow man crosses at the walk at Grace Street, and he feels a rage building in his throat. It occurs to him that he has never met anyone capable of true violence, other than witnessing a college bar fight or two. What if this whole time that's who Cammie was, someone capable of the kind of violence you see on the news, the senseless, random kind? When he finally pulls into Shelby's driveway he texts to say that he's there, and that he'll circle the house before coming to the front door. He doesn't want Cammie to hurt Shelby, but he also doesn't want to have to hurt Cammie.

He takes the big flashlight he keeps in the truck for emergencies and briefly considers calling the police. What if he can't handle whatever he finds? He pulls out his phone and dials 9-1, but then stops. This is ridiculous. He can walk around the house first before making a potential nuisance call. He shines the flashlight on every inch of the property. He checks under the barbecue, sees bunny eyes in the cedar hedges; he opens the shed and sees nothing but garden tools. He sees nothing unusual until he's on the front porch and steps down on something hard—the weird dog statue has been blown apart somehow; there's a severed ceramic collie head and pieces of its body in front of the door. Nothing else looks off. Maybe whatever happened to the dog was the sound Shelby heard? Can a piece of pottery spontaneously explode? He sees the lights turn on and the front door swing open. Shelby is cradling her dog, and both have wild, wide pupils.

"I think she came by and shot your dog statue. Or broke it somehow?"

They look out onto the street. It's quiet. No sign of Cammie.

"OMG, do you think she's threatening Coach Taylor?!"

"Leslie said she used to ruin things of hers when she got mad at her. Maybe it's like that?"

They sit on the porch together, catching their breath. Shelby begins to giggle, and then erupts into a full-body laugh. "This whole thing is crazy. I feel like an utter lunatic. I have anxiety disorder but I have never been that scared in my life. I can't thank you enough for coming. I didn't know who else to call."

"We're in this together, kid," he says.

"What should we do?"

"I'm not sure. Do you feel safe now?"

"I don't know. I know—I know what to do." She takes out her phone and starts texting as Gibson clicks the flashlight on and off.

Shelby shows him a text she's written to Cammie: *Why did you destroy Nina?*

"Should I send it? I know it's pointless to ask, but part of me still thinks the old Cammie is there somehow and will answer and just be normal again."

"Nah, she's gone. But I know what you mean. I have to keep reminding myself that she was never who she pretended to be."

"What would you have done if Cammie had accepted our help? Would you have taken her back?"

Gibson shakes his head. "I have no idea. Part of me, I think, didn't think it was possible."

Gibson takes her phone and suggests they block Cammie on everything.

"We'll feel better, I think, if we do."

"I can't. I have to know what happens. I can't just pretend it's all over and resolved."

She presses send on the text.

Before Shelby goes back to bed, she makes up the couch for Gibson. They both scroll through their phones, instinctively looking for her, trying to solve the mystery that can't be solved.

EPILOGUE

As quickly as Cammie showed up in their lives, she is gone. She is supposed to work a job for Olive and then never shows up on the first day. She blocks them both on social media before they have a chance to block her.

After the failed intervention, Gibson decides to take action in his life. He rejoins the gym. He books a vacation. He signs up for Tinder. He matches with a woman named Jen who is newly divorced and open to anything. They have a coffee date. Then a few drinks. She's very attractive and interesting but Gibson cannot seem to access the feelings required to actually date her. At the end of their drinks date she says, "I'm going to level with you. I just want to hook up with someone nice, just to, like, get it over with and see how it feels. I'm not ready for anything serious. Would you be game?"

He appreciates her honesty and goes home with her. She has a condo on the lake, half unpacked, with generic furniture. Their kissing isn't that compatible, but she doesn't seem to mind, and when she starts taking off his clothes he doesn't protest. The sex they have is enjoyable, but when he starts walking home along Spadina, by the time he gets to Dundas he had almost forgotten where he was coming from. When he hooked up with Cammie he would walk into traffic and blank out at intersections just from the memory of something she did or said. Compared to sex with Cammie, the hookup was like an entirely different activity.

———————

Shelby messages Leslie to ask her if she'd like to try another intervention, but she replies a week later with a shrug emoji and the words *Why bother*. A few months later Leslie posts photos of a family reunion, and there is Cammie, smiling and holding up a baby niece. Soon after that Leslie unfriends both Gibson and Shelby. Shelby is initially obsessed with finding out who Cammie is conning next, trying to warn them. She figures out who the tattoo artist is and writes her a long, involved email explaining that Cammie is a scammer and that she wishes she'd been warned and that she feels she has a duty to warn her. Even with the details about stealing money and the credit agencies calling her, the tattoo artist never replies. Shelby knows that if anyone asks, Cammie will have a dramatic but compelling story about both of them, that Gibson was a bad boyfriend, that Shelby was insane. She's probably told others that Shelby stole money from her. They have to make peace with the possibility that those lies are out there, that whoever she cons next will believe her.

For the next few years every time Shelby or Gibson meet someone who is charming, friendly, eager to share vulnerable details of their life early on, they stay away. They don't stay in touch but when they run into each other they hug for a long time, like they've been through a war together. Gibson falls in love again but he is always a little suspicious in ways that often drive women away. When Gibson's sister gets cancer and he sees first-hand what it looks like, he can't believe how gullible he was with Cammie. Picking her up from chemo, seeing the exhaustion on her face, the way her entire body changed, he couldn't believe that he thought the vibrant girl who took him home from the bar was in treatment for cancer.

Eventually Gibson gets engaged to a woman he dated in high school, who is kind and sentimental and the opposite of dramatic. Sometimes he finds her dull, but it's the kind of dull that's safe and it's like a weighted blanket. And when it gets to be too much he stays up late online gambling, trying to feel that extreme dopamine high he got with Cammie.

———————

Shelby tells the story of Cammie at parties, like "Did I tell you about how after Kate died, I met a con artist who lied about having cancer? Can you believe it?" And usually one person in every group can believe it, has met someone who told a similar story, but everyone else is captivated. She leaves out the part where she lost her job and didn't leave the house for a year, and eventually went to inpatient treatment for anxiety disorder and still can't work a full-time job.

One night she is walking Coach Taylor by the beach and finds two abandoned puppies. She takes them home and fosters them, and the following week a feral cat gives birth under the bushes in her backyard and she takes them in too. She makes silly videos about it on TikTok. People start calling her about animals they find. Six months later she realizes she is running an animal rescue. She draws a logo and names it Kate's Rescue and dedicates most of her time to learning how best to care for every new foster.

Gibson invites Shelby to Julian's Labour Day barbecue every year, and the second year she sits down next to a charming person named CJ, Julian and Kelly's dog walker. CJ has a salt-and-pepper crew cut and a soft manner, and six months later CJ and Shelby buy a small farm north of the city to run the rescue together.

One afternoon they're at the Ikea in North York buying another couch they hope the dogs won't destroy when Shelby's heart stops at the sight of Cammie, still beautiful as ever, walking arm in arm with an actor she recognizes from a CBC show. Cammie has a handbag slung over her shoulder worth more than Shelby's car. A few months later she sees Cammie on TV, one of the hosts of a group talk show. She speaks with a curious English accent but it's definitely her. She calls Gibson immediately. They agree she was a social climber, all about social status and money, and in some way it makes sense.

Shelby sometimes daydreams that Cammie is found out, that there will be a long *Toronto Life* article one day about how she ripped people off and pretended to be someone important and finally someone she scammed got mad enough to unveil her. But it never happens. Cammie creates reality for herself, in a way that's almost admirable.

There are worse things than telling a lie. Believe me. I've lived through them. Learning to tell people what they need to hear, exactly when they most need to hear it? That's a life skill. That's mogul shit. It's also charity in some cases. Like Gibson? That man needed love. He was on the edge. He needed to be needed by someone, to rebuild his core, his self-esteem. I gave him a gift. He could save me and feel good about himself. I mean, man, I did love him. He could really kiss, and kissing is important. We could have lasted a long time. I think we had what it takes. But power got in the way. It always does. But lying on its own? Who does it really hurt? It's what CEOs do. It's how you get what you need in life. Everyone pretends that their reality is the only one.

Women like Shelby thrive on hysteria. She is never calm. I bet she was anxious even when Kate was alive. Maybe Kate died because God or whoever was like, *This bitch needs a break from her crazy wife.* Who really knows? I mean, she was kind to me. She bought me things and took care of me like a mother would—not my mother, of course, she's too selfish, but Shelby was good at being a mom type. My sister says I'm always harder on women.

But their weaknesses bother me more than men's. They should know better. Men are just adorable idiots.

I've only met a few truly good people in my life. I thought Shelby was good at first. But I was wrong. Carol Jo is good-hearted. A real angel. My dad would never hurt a fly. Sure, he's got his problems, but who doesn't? He never got a fair shake in life, just like Nana says. People make mistakes. And so many people are just waiting around ready to judge your every word, your every action, like my mom. But we don't all start out with the same amount of everything. Imagine if I'd started out with what Shelby had, a house her parents just gave her, a dad who'd come over whenever she needed him, even when she was in her thirties. She's wasted so many opportunities. It's a real shame.

I know you think the cancer was fake now. But it wasn't. I learned young that you have to face the worst things on your own, or else you'll be indebted to others your whole life. The only one who saw me on treatment days, when I was almost willing to let God take me, was a nurse named Joanne who would bring me homemade jam every week. I could let Joanne see me that way because she'd never know me outside the hospital. I still go visit her sometimes. I drop off presents for her kids on their birthdays. She always says, "Oh, Cammie, my fighter, you're here to brighten my day, aren't you?" And I am. I do. It's important to give back to those who stick by you. It's all we have in life—loyalty.

ACKNOWLEDGEMENTS

Thank you to my agent, Samantha Haywood; my editors, Iris Tupholme, Anne Speyer, and Andra Miller; my publicist at Harper-Collins, Rebecca Silver; and the publicity team at Ballantine. Thank you to my friends Ange, Lisa, Will, Andrea, Marcilyn, Paul, and Matt, and everyone who was around in 2007 to listen to me when I figured out the truth.

ABOUT THE AUTHOR

ZOE WHITTALL is the author of the bestselling novels *The Spectacular* ("A knockout."—*Oprah Daily*), *The Best Kind of People* (finalist for the Scotiabank Giller Prize), *Holding Still for as Long as Possible* (winner of a Lambda Literary Award), and more. She has published three volumes of poetry and worked as a TV writer on *Degrassi: The Next Generation*, *Schitt's Creek*, and the *Baroness von Sketch Show*. She lives in Prince Edward County, Ontario.

ABOUT THE TYPE

This book was set in Scala, a typeface designed by Martin
Majoor in 1991. It was originally designed for a music
company in the Netherlands and then was published by
the international type house FSI FontShop. Its distinctive
extended serifs add to the articulation of the letterforms
to make it a very readable typeface.